SONANCE

AN ECHO TRILOGY NOVELLA DUET

LINDSEY FAIRLEIGH

RUBUS PRESS

Copyright © 2021 by Lindsey Fairleigh
All rights reserved.

This book is a work of fiction. All characters, organizations, and events are products of the author's imaginations or are used fictitiously. No reference to any real person, living or dead, is intended or should be inferred.

Editing by Sarah Kolb-Williams
www.kolbwilliams.com

9781539568124

ALSO BY LINDSEY FAIRLEIGH

KAT DUBOIS CHRONICLES

Ink Witch

Outcast

Underground

Soul Eater

Judgement

Afterlife

ECHO TRILOGY

Echo in Time

Resonance

Time Anomaly

Dissonance

Ricochet Through Time

ATLANTIS LEGACY

Sacrifice of the Sinners

Legacy of the Lost

Fate of the Fallen

Dreams of the Damned

Song of the Soulless

ALLWORLD ONLINE

AO: Pride & Prejudice

AO: The Wonderful Wizard of Oz

Vertigo

THE ENDING SERIES

The Ending Beginnings: Omnibus Edition

After The Ending

Into The Fire

Out Of The Ashes

Before The Dawn

World Before

THE ENDING LEGACY

World After

For more information on Lindsey and her books:

www.lindseyfairleigh.com

Join Lindsey's mailing list to stay up to date on releases

AND to get a FREE copy of *Sacrifice of the Sinners.*

www.lindseyfairleigh.com/sacrifice

To read Lindsey's books as she writes them, check her out on Patreon:

www.patreon.com/lindseyfairleigh

SONANCE TABLE OF CONTENTS

RESONANCE

DISSONANCE

RESONANCE

1

PUSH & PULL

"I'm almost ready!" I called to Marcus from the tiny bathroom attached to our bedroom. The building the Council of Seven used as their headquarters in Florence was a stunning Renaissance palazzo, filled with all the high-ceilinged chambers, arches, gilding, and frescoes one could ask for, but the living quarters on its top two floors were definitely on the small side. And small living quarters, though exquisitely furnished, meant itty-bitty bathrooms.

"Take your time, Little Ivanov. The meeting with Sotheby's isn't for another two hours."

Since Florence was one of the few Nejeret-heavy cities where Marcus *didn't* own a house, he'd decided it was the perfect time to meet with an agent to start shopping for our very first Lex-and-Marcus Firenze home. I caught myself grinning like a fool in the mirror hanging over the pedestal sink. Excitement shone in my eyes, making my carmine irises appear even more crimson than usual.

And only adding to my giddiness was the fact that this would be my first time actually leaving the palazzo's heavily guarded grounds. The gardens might've been just as wondrous as the palace itself, but they were surrounded by walls, and even though I was permitted to wander through them without any of my guards, I was still separated from the outside world. I'd never been to Florence before, and today's outing would finally give me a chance to see some of the sights I'd only heard about since waking from my regenerative slumber: the Ponte Vecchio bridge, the Duomo and the other basilicas, the Fountain of Neptune . . .

I was ridiculously eager—and, as such, spending way too much time on my appearance. For whatever reason, primping tended to steady my nerves.

Staring into the mirror once more, I finished my makeup with a dab of my favorite vanilla-plum lip balm, then held my eyes wide and tried not to blink as I put in my plain-old-brown-colored contacts. I plucked the necklace hanging from one of the mirror's many flourishes and headed out to the bedroom.

"Help, please." I held the necklace out to Marcus, who was sitting on the foot of the bed in nothing but charcoal-gray slacks and an unbuttoned white dress shirt. His eyes were closed, and his body was completely still; he didn't even appear to be breathing.

For nearly a minute, I watched him, studied the strong, clean lines of his face, the bronzed skin and contours of muscle visible through the opening in his shirt, thinking it was unfair for any living being to be so inhumanly beautiful. Especially when, underneath all of that enticing flesh, there was enough charisma, sharp intellect, and passion for a dozen men. But he wasn't a dozen men; he was Marcus, ancient and world-weary Marcus, and he was all mine.

Finally, he took a slow, deep breath. I sighed. He was in At-qed, the hypometabolic state a Nejeret went into when his ba left his body to wander through the At, the very fabric of space and time, to view events of the past, present, and possible futures. And Marcus's ba—his *soul*—was in the At . . . again.

In the week since the encounter with Set in Hatchepsut's mortuary temple, his need to check the At, to test its stability and measure the intensity of the Nothingness that threatened to overtake it, had increased to the point of obsession. It wasn't that he *needed* to do it. Dozens of other Nejerets had been assigned that task specifically, but he didn't seem to trust their observations. At every possible moment, he plunged into the At, and it was getting a tad irritating. Especially considering that *I* was *avoiding* the At; after the months I'd spent in there as Set's prisoner, I wanted to keep my ba safe and sound in my body as much as possible.

There was only one surefire way to draw Marcus back to his body. Back to me.

"Marcus," I said in a singsong voice. Hitching up the skirt of my white linen sundress, I crawled onto the bed and straddled his legs. I slipped my hands under his shirt and ran my fingertips over the ridges of muscle on his abdomen and chest, then back down until my fingertips touched his belt buckle. I started to unfasten it. "You know, you should *really* be more careful about where you leave your body . . . who knows what someone might do with it." Touching my lips to the honey-colored skin at the crook of his neck, I smiled. "When Marcus's ba is away, Lex will play . . ."

Marcus inhaled suddenly, exhaling with a rough chuckle. "Ah . . . Little Ivanov, I see you're ready." I didn't miss his double entendre as his hands slid up my thighs, and he grasped my hips, pressing me against him more firmly.

"Always . . ."

Again, he chuckled. "Have I been neglecting you?"

I nodded against his neck, whimpering when I tried to move against him but couldn't. His hold on my hips was relentless.

"Hmmm . . . I must think long and hard on how I can remedy my poor treatment of you."

An eager grin spread across my face, until someone knocked on the door. My grin withered.

"Grandfather?" It was Vali, a mountainous man who was one of Marcus's myriad of Nejeret grandchildren, and also one of my head bodyguards. "I apologize for interrupting, but there is a phone call for you—someone from the Galleria dell'Accademia here in Florence. He says it's urgent."

A growl of frustration rumbled in Marcus's chest as his fingers unclenched from my hips and he stood, setting me on my feet. He placed his hands on either side of my face and stared into my eyes. His pupils slowly constricted as he restrained his desire, obsidian giving way to his black-rimmed golden irises. "A thousand apologies, Little Ivanov." He kissed me, the lightest brush of his silken lips against mine. "I will make amends for my recent transgressions . . . soon." He kissed me again, the light pressure deepening with promise.

I exhaled as he pulled away and headed for the door. He opened it with one sharp jerk.

Vali nodded at me in greeting, and I offered him a small smile as he handed Marcus a cordless phone.

Marcus turned away from the doorway and, staring at the gold-embossed scarlet wallpaper behind the mahogany headboard, raised the phone to his ear. "This is Marcus Bahur. To whom am I speaking?" He pulled the phone away when a man on the other end started speaking, his voice far too loud for Marcus's sensitive hearing. Luckily, since my hearing was almost as heightened as his, I could hear the other man's accented voice quite clearly.

"Superintendent Pietro Gaspari, signore. I am calling you about the Michelangelo sculpture you have so generously loaned to dell'Accademia . . ."

Marcus brought the receiver closer to his mouth. "*La Donna Triste . . . ?*"

"Yes. I am sorry, signore, but it would appear there was a break-in over the night, and she has been . . . defaced."

Marcus's left hand clenched into such a tight fist that his knuckles blanched. "In what way was *La Donna* defaced?"

"A symbol was etched into her chest, directly over her heart."

Marcus closed his eyes for several long seconds, taking slow, even breaths. "I see. Grazie, Signor Gaspari. I'm certain you will not fault me for wishing to reclaim the sculpture for safekeeping. I shall be there to make arrangements for her transportation shortly."

"I understand. I will be waiting to attend to you. Again, signore, my sincerest apologies . . ."

The call ended, and Marcus handed the phone back to Vali.

I took a single step toward Marcus. "So, we'll head over to the Accademia before the meeting?"

"*I* will go, Little Ivanov." He avoided meeting my eyes. "*You* will stay here, and I will return to fetch you before our meeting with the agent, when more of your guards are available."

I stared up at the plaster moldings on the ceiling and took a deep breath, then focused once again on the most obstinate man in the world. "Marcus . . . you're doing that thing again." He had a bad habit of trying to order me around.

Frustration flashed in those golden eyes. "There is no need for your presence at dell'Accademia. It is merely an administrative issue."

"Then send Carlisle . . . or Dom," I countered.

"It is a matter I would greatly prefer to attend to myself."

"Then I'm coming with you," I said, forcing a bright smile. "Vali and Sandra were planning on accompanying us later anyway, so there should be no problem having them join us now . . . right, Vali?" I didn't look away from Marcus.

Vali cleared his throat. "If that is your wish, Meswett."

My smile widened. There were a few perks to being the

prophesied savior of an entire species of godlike beings, one being that my "suggestions" carried a whole lot of weight. "It is. Thank you, Vali," I said, watching Marcus's jaw clench and unclench and his nostrils flare repeatedly. "Please go inform Sandra."

Vali didn't waste any time in leaving us. He shut the door quietly, and I listened as his footsteps retreated too quickly for a walk.

Marcus took a deep breath, exhaling heavily. "I dislike the idea of you leaving the palazzo without a full retinue of guards." He shook his head. "If something were to happen to you, I . . ." My will to *not* be left behind for the umpteenth time since we'd been in Florence threatened to crumble under the sheer force of concern shining in Marcus's eyes.

I straightened my spine and held my head high. "And if I stay here, safe and sound behind high walls and locked doors, but something happens to you . . . then what happens to me?" I closed the distance between us in two long strides and reached up, placing my hand against his contoured cheek. "The results are the same either way, Marcus; we made sure of that the moment we sealed our bond. Like it or not"—I let one corner of my mouth quirk up in a crooked smile—"and I think you like it . . . you're stuck with me."

Marcus's lips twitched. "It infuriates me when you use logical arguments."

I grinned, stood on my tiptoes, and pressed my lips against his.

Marcus's arms were around me in an instant, the fingers of one hand splayed against the small of my back while his other hand gripped the back of my neck. He took control of the embrace, and it was control I relinquished willingly, simply trying to hold onto sanity as he unleashed a thunderstorm of a kiss. Sometimes, I was convinced that Marcus's angry kisses were my favorite.

It was short, but far from sweet, and when he pulled away, I was left gasping for air. "Well . . . that was . . . nice," I said, smoothing down my hair and clearing my throat.

Marcus smirked and raised one eyebrow.

Heat flushed my neck and cheeks. "Yeah, so, um . . ." I cleared my throat again and held the necklace out to him. "Please?"

He accepted the necklace, holding it up so the pendant dangled in front of his face. It was a three-thousand-year-old lapis lazuli falcon about the size of a house key and had been affixed in a silver setting to convert it into a pendant. Marcus had given it to me the previous night, almost looking bashful as he opened a tiny wooden jewelry box and said, "A falcon for my she-falcon."

"Do you truly like it?" he asked me now.

I turned around so he could secure the clasp behind my neck. The pendant settled against my breastbone, and I touched my fingertips to its cool, smooth surface. To wear something that symbolized Marcus—Heru—so close to my heart . . . "Marcus, I love it." My voice sounded thick, and I blinked rapidly and cleared my throat.

Marcus pressed his lips to the base of my neck, just above the chain's clasp. "Then I am pleased." He placed his hands on my shoulders and turned me around, scanning me from head to toe. The faintest line appeared between his eyebrows.

"What? Is something wrong with what I'm wearing?" I glanced down. The white linen of my sundress was a little rumpled from what had *almost* happened a few minutes earlier, but it wasn't stained or torn, and I couldn't find any fault with the silver-embellished sandals on my feet or the slender leather belt cinched around my waist. I smoothed my hands down the skirt of my dress compulsively and repeated, "What?"

Marcus frowned. "I'm not sure, I just—" His eyes returned to my face, and he shook his head. "A trick of the mind, I think." His lips spread into a heartbreakingly handsome smile. "I blame you. You fill my head with such strange fanciful notions every day . . . such impossible dreams every night."

My eyebrows rose. "Right . . ."

Again, Marcus shook his head, laughing softly to himself. He quickly buttoned his shirt and slipped on his shoes before taking my hand and threading our fingers together. "Come, Little Ivanov. It would seem we have a busy day ahead of us."

2

AMONG & APART

Since the Galleria dell'Accademia wasn't far from the Council's palazzo—just across the Fiume Arno, the river splitting Florence in two, and several blocks to the north in the heart of the city—we decided to walk. I was utterly delighted. Sotheby's was far enough away from the palazzo that I'd expected I would only get to see Florence through a rolled-up car window. But now, since foot traffic would likely make driving to the Accademia take longer than walking, I had a chance to be a genuine, slow-walking, gaping-at-my-surroundings tourist. I just wished I had a camera.

I was in a state of awe as we stepped onto the south end of the Ponte Vecchio bridge, the medieval bridge famous for still being lined by tiny shops as it would have been hundreds of years ago; only Marcus's hold on my hand kept me moving forward. It was the beginning of summer, and despite it still being relatively early in the morning, the pedestrian-only bridge was packed with tourists on either side, most pausing every few yards to stare into the window display of the next tiny boutique jewelry shop in an endless line of nearly identical shops.

Lucky for our foursome—Vali, Sandra, Marcus, and me—

there was a relatively clear path down the center of the bridge, and we were able to make our way across fairly quickly. Vali took point, which seemed to entail looking everywhere at once while taking momentary breaks every now and again to stare down anyone who'd taken an interest in Marcus and me. Sandra, a childlike woman who was at least as deadly as Vali and also one of Marcus's grandchildren, trailed a short distance behind us. With a brief glance over my shoulder, I saw that she was doing essentially the same thing as Vali, with just a touch more glaring.

While we crossed the bridge, I gawked at the scene around us, but when we neared its end, I turned my attention to Marcus and gave his hand a squeeze. "So . . . you own a Michelangelo sculpture."

"I do," he said, scanning the myriad of people and stone and stucco buildings with almost as intense a focus as Vali and Sandra.

I held back a smile. "Tell me, Marcus—*why* do you own a Michelangelo sculpture?"

The corner of his mouth lifted, but he narrowed his eyes and pretended to frown as he continued to watch our surroundings. "Well, I suppose it's because I quite enjoy the way it looks."

A soft laugh glided up my throat. "And *how* do you own a Michelangelo sculpture?"

I was expecting him to say something along the lines of "I bought it." But that would have been far too simple. I was being naïve, still thinking like a human.

"I commissioned it."

I stopped mid-step at the foot of the bridge and gaped at him. "You commissioned it."

Marcus looked back at me over his shoulder, one eyebrow raised. "I did."

"From Michelangelo."

He glanced around, looking bored, but I caught that telltale twitch at the corner of his mouth. "The very one."

I held up a hand. "The same guy who made the *David* and painted the ceiling of the Sistine Chapel? We're talking about the same guy, right?"

Marcus tugged on my hand, but I refused to budge. He sighed. "Yes, Little Ivanov, we are speaking of the same man." His momentary amusement fizzled away, and he returned to scanning the people around us. "May we please continue? I'm eager to assess the damage and conclude this unwelcome business as quickly as possible."

I pursed my lips and studied his tensed features. "You mean, you want to interrogate their security people and confiscate any video footage of the break-in as soon as possible . . . so you can hunt down whoever vandalized your precious sculpture and make them kneel before you and beg for your forgiveness right before you do something exceptionally painful to them, right?"

Marcus met first Vali's eyes, then Sandra's, nodding once to each of them, before releasing my hand and turning to face me fully. He stepped as close as possible without actually touching me, and leaned in until his lips were a hairsbreadth from my ear. "You're right. I will interrogate the Accademia's security personnel, I will confiscate their video footage, and I will track down the offending party." He paused, inhaled, held his breath. I did the same. "But you're wrong about one thing; the only person I desire to have kneeling before me, Little Ivanov, is you, and I promise you that it is for a reason that has nothing to do with pain."

Suddenly parched, I swallowed. Several times. "Oh, well . . ." I cleared my throat. "I see."

Marcus pulled away, his eyes glinting wickedly. "Now, may we continue?"

At a loss for words and unable to look away from those golden pools of sin, I nodded and let Marcus lead me forward once more.

A short way from the bridge, the street widened and the crowd thinned noticeably. We passed shop fronts in the bottom floors of antiquated four- and five-story buildings, carrying everything from shoes, hats, and dresses to sunglasses and jewelry, as well as cafés, gelaterias, banks, and even a pharmacy. An enormous open-air building came into view on the left side of the street, hosting a bustling outdoor market that looked like it could provide hours of enjoyment.

My steps slowed as I imagined wandering from stall to stall, looking at scarves and trinkets and leather bags. It wasn't that I wanted to buy anything. I already had everything I needed, and I'd never been prone to excess; I didn't even have a car back in Seattle, and I had one, maybe two really nice dresses. But I wanted the experience, the memory, something I could keep with me forever. I just wanted to feel like I was actually *here*.

"The Loggia del Porcellino," Marcus said, catching my line of sight and what was probably a ridiculous look of longing. "Perhaps we'll stop by when we're finished, if we have time," he added as we headed away from the haggling hubbub. "I forget that this is your first time in Firenze, and that you've spent most of it locked up inside the palazzo." He apologized with a smile and a squeeze of my hand. "Most would have complained by now."

I met his eyes and returned his smile. "I enjoy the gardens. They're peaceful, which is surprising given how close they are to all of this." I gestured to the seemingly endless sea of pedestrians.

"You're mastering the art of deflection, Little Ivanov." He sent me an approving glance. "An important skill if you're to be a successful leader among our people. But that is aside from the point—until we leave for Cairo, I shall show you as much as I can of the city, and we'll begin tonight, after we finish with the Sotheby's agent. How does that sound?"

I beamed at him. "It sounds fantastic, Marcus."

3

WITHIN & WITHOUT

The entrance to the Galleria dell'Accademia, where Michelangelo's notorious *Statue of David* was on display, was remarkably unassuming. The simple, oversized wooden door in the stucco wall was one in an intermittent line of others just like it, and it lent the Accademia an air of humility that seemed at odds with the long column of people milling along the exterior of the museum, waiting to enter. We neither waited nor milled.

Marcus guided me through a break in the crowd and straight into the Accademia through the exit, Sandra and Vali flanking us. Embarrassment heated my cheeks as I imagined being one of the hundreds of people waiting in line, watching someone else barge in through the back door.

"Hey!" a woman shouted. "You can't do that. Harry, they can't just do that! It's not fair!"

Pausing, I glanced over my shoulder and spotted the woman; she was poking a rather apathetic-looking man with one hand and pointing at us with the other. My flush burned hotter, and I offered her a tight-lipped smile.

Marcus gave my hand a squeeze before releasing it, and I looked away from the outraged woman.

"Ah . . . Signor Bahur, my name is Giovanni. I was sent to wait for you." Our greeter was a young man with a head of curly, dark hair and pleasant, wide-set features. He shook Marcus's hand with gusto.

"I was expecting Superintendent Pietro Gaspari to meet me," Marcus said as Giovanni released his hand.

"Ah, yes, Signor Gaspari is very sorry he cannot be here; he was called away for family business . . . very important . . ."

"I hope everything is alright." Though Marcus's words displayed a polite level of concern, his voice was bland.

Giovanni bowed his head. "Yes, yes, I believe so, but do not worry. Signor Gaspari called in a replacement to handle the situation for him, and we already moved *La Donna Triste* to a restricted area upstairs as soon as we noticed . . . it."

"I'm pleased to hear it," Marcus said, sounding about as far from pleased as someone could be. He extended his arm toward a pair of fogged glass doors. "May we proceed?"

But Giovanni didn't see Marcus's gesture; he was too busy staring at me, his lips parted and his eyes wide. "*Madonna . . . la somiglianza . . .*" He looked like he'd seen a ghost.

Marcus cleared his throat, and I glanced at him in time to see him giving Giovanni his equivalent of a death stare. "*Una coincidenza, niente di piú.*"

Though Italian wasn't one of the languages I'd studied as an archaeologist specializing in ancient Egypt, I was familiar with enough of it that I could catch the gist of the exchange. Something about my appearance was shocking to Giovanni, and Marcus was claiming there was some sort of a "coincidence."

Eyebrows raised, I looked from Marcus to the young man and back and cleared my throat, loudly. It was practically a cough.

Marcus's eyes flicked to mine for the briefest moment.

"I apologize, signora," Giovanni rushed to say. "Your beauty stunned me for a moment, is all."

I sent Marcus a sidelong glance, but he wouldn't meet my eyes. "I'm sure . . ."

"Come, come . . . I take you to *La Donna*." Giovanni ushered Marcus and me toward the doors, Sandra and Vali following close behind us.

We entered a long, high-ceilinged gallery filled with people, most concentrated near a rotunda at the far end, where the *David* held court, towering over them. Others stood in clusters all along the gallery's walls, staring up at the few enormous paintings, which practically dripped religious iconography, or resting on the built-in mahogany benches below the Renaissance masterpieces. I stared around as Giovanni guided us through the mass of people, heading straight for the *David*.

But impressive as the famous statue of the giant-killer was, it didn't hold my attention for long. The handful of huge, unfinished marble sculptures scattered along the sides of the gallery captivated me completely. Each depicted a nude man, and though each was utterly unique, they all shared a sense of being trapped within the stone. It was like their creator had been attempting to set them free, but he'd given up, and now they were stuck, encased in stone . . . forever. When I said as much to Marcus, he called ahead to Giovanni in Italian and drew me closer to the nearest partially revealed male form, which displayed only a pair of rough-hewn legs, a muscular torso, and part of an arm.

"Which is precisely why they are known as *The Prisoners* to many," Marcus said as he laced our fingers together.

I glanced down at the placard. "*Atlas*." It seemed a fitting name for the slightly hunched over figure, though rather than holding the world, it appeared that the world was holding the poor, trapped soul. "They're beautiful . . ." I looked at Marcus, then continued studying the unfinished sculpture. "And a little disturbing."

Marcus nodded. "An accurate assessment, in my opinion." Only when I felt him tug on my hand did I realize he'd started walking away.

I resisted, feeling an uncomfortable kinship with this half-formed stone man.

"Come on, Little Ivanov." Marcus gave my hand another tug. "The crowd has thinned."

As I walked away, I continued to stare at *Atlas* for a few more heartbeats before turning my attention to the sole statue in the rotunda ahead. There was only a scattering of people around him now, as though a guided tour group had just moved on.

Marcus stopped near the low glass barrier surrounding the *David* and said something else to Giovanni, who was waiting partway down the narrower gallery to the left of the rotunda.

I stepped in front of Marcus, moving as close to the barrier as possible to get a better look at the sculpture. I stared at the *David* for minutes, studying the precision and delicacy with which he'd been formed and finished. He was so perfect, so life-like, but at the same time, subtle things were off about him. His lowered hand was in my direct line of sight, and once my eyes latched onto it, I couldn't tear them away.

"What do you think?" Marcus asked from behind me.

"His hand . . ." I shook my head. "It's so big—compared to the rest of him, I mean. It's *really* big." Distractingly so.

Marcus moved closer to me, wrapping his arms around my waist and resting his check against my hair. "It was for perspective."

I relaxed against him, no longer so distracted . . . at least, not by the *David*'s huge hand. "Is that so?"

"*David*, here, was originally intended to decorate the roofline of the Duomo; from so far below, he would have appeared quite proportionate." Marcus paused, taking a long, slow inhale. He exhaled with a groan and tightened his hold around my waist. "It's not uncommon knowledge. I'm surprised you didn't already know."

I sighed and leaned my head back against his shoulder. "This is what I know about Michelangelo—" I held up my hand to tick points off with my fingers and said, "Renaissance, the *Statue of David*, the Sistine Chapel . . . and that's about it." I dropped my hand. "I never really studied the Renaissance, not after high school," I added, wrinkling my nose. "It just felt too recent."

"Your preference for the ancient world has left you ignorant of the more recent past, Little Ivanov." He chuckled. "Though I must admit that I appreciate your preference for the ancient—it's benefitted *me* greatly…and often."

I closed my eyes in an effort to shield myself from the truth behind his words: that he was as ancient as the people I loved to study. It was useless. I could no more ignore the fact that Marcus was over four thousand years old than I could avoid the possibility that one day, I might be just as ancient.

Marcus must have caught a glimpse of my expression, because he moved his lips closer to my ear and whispered, "Let go of what you were, Lex. Embrace what you *are*."

Were and *are* . . . that was the problem. I opened my eyes and craned my neck so I could see his face. "Why can't I be both?" I wanted to hold on to my humanity, to continue to appreciate each moment for what it was—unique and precious. Each moment would only happen once, each second would only pass once, no matter how many times I ventured into the At to watch a replay. I wanted to *live* my life, not watch it. An echo wasn't the same; it wasn't *real*. And above all, I wanted to avoid the ennui that seemed to infect so many Nejerets over time.

A slight frown touched Marcus's lips, and there was a tightness around his eyes that hadn't been there a moment before, but he didn't respond to my question. Instead, he nodded to my two bodyguards, who were standing on opposite sides of the domed chamber, their eyes assessing everything. "Stay out here with Vali and Sandra while I take care of this business. I'll only be a moment."

"But—"

Marcus turned me around to face him fully and pressed his lips to mine, kissing me deeply. A child giggled, the sound reverberating within the rotunda, and I broke the kiss. My cheeks were on fire.

"Go," Marcus said. "Spend some more time with *Atlas* and the other *Prisoners*. We won't be able to linger afterward . . ."

Biting my lip, I glanced over Marcus's shoulder at the unfinished statues and nodded. There was just something so enthralling about them.

Marcus pressed another, chaste kiss to my lips before turning and striding away with Giovanni. I watched them walk up the gallery until they passed through a doorway into another area and were out of sight.

I wasn't the least bit surprised to find Vali approaching as I made my way back toward *Atlas*. When neither Marcus nor Dominic was by my side, Vali was always there. His sheer size, all clearly muscle mass, worked as an excellent deterrent for anyone who was even considering approaching me with the intent to harm, while Sandra could just as easily hang back, blend in, look harmless . . . *and* catch anyone intending to harm me from afar.

I met Vali's ice-blue eyes as he fell in step beside me, matching my meandering pace. "Have you been here before?"

"Yes, Meswett. I served as a Council guard for years; it's what I was doing before I swore my oath to protect you."

"Hmmm," I said, glancing at him with a thoughtful frown. Vali was a gentle giant, at least where I was concerned, but he was also a man of few words. Despite the amount of time we spent in each other's presence, I didn't know much about him.

"And whenever Heru was in town for Council business, he would make a point to come here to visit *La Donna*, which makes more sense now"—his eyes touched my face, sliding away quickly—"and I was his usual companion."

My frown deepened as we took up a position off to the side of *Atlas*, me studying Vali's pale, stony face, and Vali scowling as he scanned the museum-goers around us. "*Why* does it make more sense now?" I asked him.

"It isn't my place to say, Meswett. You'll have to ask Heru."

I crossed my arms and shook my head, cursing myself for being a pushover and staying behind when I should have insisted on going with Marcus. I was getting the rather clear impression that he didn't want me to see this sculpture of his, this "sad woman," and I was tempted to march after him and Giovanni to shed some light on the mystery. Thanks to my Nejerette senses, I could still hear them exchanging words as they moved further away; it wouldn't be hard to find them. Or, I realized, I could always slip into the At and take a peek that way . . .

I cleared my throat and uncrossed my arms. I definitely wasn't ready to risk another trip into the At. Not yet, not so soon after . . . everything.

Looking back up at Vali, I let the subject of *La Donna* drop. It wasn't his fault Marcus was being, well, Marcus. "Do you have a favorite *Prisoner*, Vali?"

He blinked, like he was surprised by my question. After a moment, he nodded to the sculpture opposite *Atlas*, a more fully formed but still rough-hewn man whose neck was bent in an uncomfortable-looking angle. "*The Bearded Slave*," he said. "He reminds me of my grandfather—my mother's human father, not Heru. He was a great Viking explorer, an excellent warrior." His lips curved into the tiniest possible smile as he allowed himself a stolen moment of nostalgia.

A few seconds later, he was back to scanning the people

around us. A new wave was filling the gallery, and I figured it was just another guided tour group. I noticed the woman who'd been so outraged when we'd slipped in through the exit, five policemen trailing behind her. When our eyes met, she grinned.

I was about to mention her odd reaction to Vali when my ears picked up on a familiar, unwelcome voice coming from the direction Marcus and Giovanni had gone, just barely audible over the crowd: Sara, a woman who knew Marcus with intimate familiarity.

". . . be here, I made special arrangements to be the one to assist you." She sounded just as sultry and overtly provocative as she had when I'd eavesdropped on her and Marcus meeting in his tent months ago. It was the same tone that had launched me into an instinctive Nejerette reaction, resulting in me threatening her life if she ever came near Marcus again—and claiming him as the Nejeret equivalent of my husband.

Narrowing my eyes, I scowled. That same instinct was kicking in again, making me hunger for Sara's terror, thirst for her tears. Oblivious to my immediate surroundings, I spun on my heel and started to head back up the gallery to track them down, but the crowd had thickened to the point that I had to push between people to get anywhere.

"I thought you returned to London," I heard Marcus say. He had to know I could hear them, had to suspect I was on my way *to* them. "You should have stayed there."

"Oh, I did go to London—and I made a very interesting new friend who, coincidentally, knew a bit about our little falling out and your new *woman*. He made me an offer I couldn't refuse, and . . ."

I'd made my way through most of the rotunda when a large hand wrapped around my upper arm, jerking me to a halt. I turned to tell Vali to let me go.

And snapped my mouth shut almost as soon as I'd opened it. Instead of Vali's pale blue eyes, I was staring into the hazel eyes of a stranger. A large, leering, male stranger. A heartbeat later, I recognized him; he was the bored man the outraged woman had been poking just outside.

He yanked me backward, into the edge of the crowd, and leaned in closer. "I told Set this would be easy . . ."

4

TRY & FAIL

I twisted, trying to yank my arm out of Bored Man's grip. He was human—which gave me an advantage, since my Nejerette regenerative abilities kept me in prime shape—but he was also *far* bigger and stronger than me.

But strength and size weren't everything.

I gritted my teeth. "If you don't let go right now—"

Bored Man sneered and pulled me closer. "You'll what? Scream? I wouldn't—Heru's in a bit of a scuffle at the moment, and a distraction could prove fatal. And blondie?" He exhaled a harsh laugh and nodded back toward the main gallery without looking that way. "Don't hold your breath, sweetheart . . . he's been detained."

My captor started to turn, likely intending to drag me down the corridor and out some back door, but he stopped short. Sandra was standing so close to him, and the area around the *David* was still so crowded with museum-goers, that nobody but me could see the needlelike blade she'd slipped between his ribs. My attempted abductor gasped and stiffened, and his legs buckled. With a groan, he collapsed to his knees on the tile floor, and his hand fell away from my arm.

"Aiutami!" Sandra cried out. *"Aiutami!"* More Italian followed, but it was too rushed for me to pick out any cognates. She grabbed my wrist and pulled me away from the buzzing crowd forming around our fallen foe and back toward the *David*—toward the gallery, where I assumed Vali was fending off the outraged woman and the five policemen, if that's even what they were.

"I told them he's having a heart attack," Sandra said. "That should clear the exit enough that I can get you away and back to the palazzo, and—"

"Sandra, no!" I dug in my heels and yanked my arm free from her small hand. The museum was filled with too much cacophony now to hear what was going on with Marcus in the restricted area upstairs; for all we knew, he could've been fending off twenty huge men at that very moment. "We can't leave Marcus. That guy said—"

"Heru can handle himself just fine." She reached for my arm again, but before she could touch me, there was a single, explosive crack of gunfire coming from one of the rooms overhead . . . where Marcus's voice had been coming from the last time I'd heard it. Sandra's eyes widened, mirroring mine.

In the blink of an eye, a misty cloud of every color exploded around me, sweeping me out of existence. The gunshot had given Nuin's borrowed powers the jumpstart they needed to kick in instinctively and sweep me to the one place I most needed to be—wherever Marcus was.

I reformed in a scene from a horror movie. A well-lit room with empty walls that had once been white and floor tiles that had once been the orange-brown of terracotta were spattered and streaked with crimson. The terracotta tiles were barely visible through all of the blood.

And then there were the bodies, broken and strewn about haphazardly like a child's discarded toys. There had to be at least a half-dozen bodies, both male and female and all dressed in jeans and black T-shirts, all except for a crumpled form in the corner, wearing black slacks and a light blue dress shirt—Giovanni. Most looked like they'd had their throats either slit open or torn out completely. The meaty, metallic smell made my stomach churn, and I salivated and swallowed compulsively, a sure sign I was on the verge of throwing up.

In the center of the room was a blood-spattered marble sculpture—*La Donna Triste,* I assumed—but I could hardly spare it a glance. Not when Marcus, covered in enough blood to make me think he'd rolled on the floor at some point during the struggle, was holding a woman against the far wall with a single hand wrapped around her neck.

Sara's rich caramel complexion and pale blouse were soiled with smudges of blood, though she wasn't wearing nearly as much as Marcus, and her dark, glossy hair was in disarray. She was holding onto Marcus's wrist with both hands as her feet dangled helplessly above the floor.

"Marcus!" I took several lurching steps toward him, my sandals slipping on the slick tile. "Jesus . . ." I had to stop partway to him to steady myself. "Are you okay? I heard a gun . . ."

Marcus released Sara, and she dropped to the floor with a splat, boneless and gasping for air. When he looked at me, his eyes were almost entirely black, only the thinnest strip of gold visible around his pupils. Nostrils flaring, he scanned me from head to toe. "You are upset." He frowned. "So they came after you, too."

He held out a hand as I neared, cautioning me not to close the final few feet separating us.

"No—yes—" I shook my head. "I mean, yes, they tried something, but it didn't work, and *of course* I'm upset—I just walked into a room filled with dead bodies and blood . . . and you're covered in blood . . ." I let out a single, despondent wail.

Looking up at the ceiling, I took a deep breath . . . which was a mistake. The air was so thick with the scent of blood I could taste it on my tongue. "Oh God . . ." I slapped my hand over my mouth, and my eyes started watering.

Marcus's focus shifted to a point behind me. "Sandra, call Carlisle. Tell him we need a clean-up team here, right now, and tell him to call Mayor Peruzzi and make arrangements for law enforcement to turn a blind eye here for the next few hours." He paused, then added, "When he confirms the Mayor's cooperation, pull the fire alarm. Also, please have Carlisle send Dom with a clean set of clothes for me."

Sandra bowed her head and pulled her phone from her back pocket, turning away as she brought it up to her ear.

Taking a deep breath, Marcus crouched in front of Sara. "Why did you make a deal with Set to arrange an ambush and try to kill me?"

Sara looked at him, blinked several times, then started to laugh; the sound was laced with hysteria. "Kill you? We didn't set this all up to *kill* you." Her wild eyes focused on me, filling with burning hatred. "We did it to *detain* you, so our other people could abduct *her*."

Marcus tilted his head to the side. "Why? What does Set want with Lex now?"

Sara's lips curved into a placid smile. "I didn't ask, because I didn't care." Her smile melted, and she glared at Marcus. "I just wanted her gone. I wanted to rip her out of your life. I wanted to hurt you the way you hurt me."

I shook my head in disgust. "What the hell is wrong with you? You made a deal with Set because—what? Because you're a woman scorned?" I flung my hand behind me, in the general direction of the blood and bodies strewn about the room. "These people are *dead* because of you." Sure, technically they were dead because of *Marcus*, but they wouldn't have been there to be slaughtered by him in the first place if not for Sara's petty deal with Set.

Sara's eyes widened, and I thought I was actually getting through to her. Until I saw her attention shift to the sculpture in the middle of the room, lingering on it for a few seconds before returning to my face. I gritted my teeth and thought, *This again?*

"Impossible," she whispered. "That can't be. It's not possible . . ." Again, her eyes shifted from me to the stone sculpture.

It was only natural to follow her line of sight.

And what I saw when I finally looked at *La Donna Triste*—when I finally *really* looked at her—made the blood and the bodies and Sara and even Marcus fall away, until it was just me and the sad woman. Until nothing else mattered.

Because she was *me*.

5

FLESH & STONE

All of the mentions of impossibility and coincidence, all of the wide-eyed looks and raised eyebrows, Vali's "makes more sense now" comment—it was all suddenly so clear.

La Donna Triste looked exactly like me.

She was sitting on her hip, her hand planted beside her, propping her up, and her lazily curled legs extended to one side. She was dangling her other hand over something, the same something she was gazing into; water, I thought, though to me it just looked like she was staring at the blood-soaked floor. A symbol had been carved into her chest, clearly not part of the original design.

And her name, *La Donna Triste*—the sad woman—truly befit her; she emanated sadness and heartbreak and eons of loss. I couldn't imagine what she'd gone through to look so incredibly sad. I couldn't imagine what *I* would have to go through to look so sad.

I blinked and shook my head as I took slow steps toward her. This wasn't a depiction of me . . . it was *not*. I had to get that through my thick skull. *La Donna Triste* was *not* a sculpture of me. She was a woman Marcus must have known centuries ago, or maybe just some stranger Michelangelo had used as a model, but she *wasn't* me; *I* was only twenty-four, and I'd certainly never met Michelangelo. Which made the whole situation so much more disturbing.

A *coincidenza,* Marcus had called it. A coincidence. A disturbing, mesmerizing, nauseating coincidence.

I sat on her pedestal and leaned in until my face was inches from hers. Subtle things were different—the arch of her right eyebrow, and the part in her hair—which made me feel a little better. At first. That momentary relief evaporated as I realized that she *would* look more right, more like me, if she were reflected. Because as she was now, it was like looking at a duplicate, at an exact, colorless copy, when what I was so used to looking at was a reflection of myself in a mirror.

Lowering my eyes to the symbol etched into her chest—a dog-like animal with pointy ears, sitting on its haunches, its forked tail held upright behind it—I felt unexpected rage burn within my veins. It was Set's symbol, the Set-animal. His people did this to her, because she looked like me. They did this to Marcus, because she looked like me. It was almost like this was Set's way to put a claim on me, through her.

"Sandra," I heard Marcus say, "please text Dom and tell him to bring a change of clothes for Lex as well. Ah, Vali, there you are . . ."

Frowning, I glanced down at myself, not understanding what was wrong with my current attire. It was when I shifted on the marble pedestal, moving away from the sad woman's face, that I felt the sticky wetness seeping through the back of my skirt. I was sitting in blood.

I managed to care for all of six seconds, until my attention touched on *La Donna Triste*'s necklace, just above the engraving of the Set-animal on her chest. The pendant hanging from an almost invisible chain was a falcon, its wings tucked in and its head turned to the side, just like the pendant hanging from a chain around my own neck. I touched my pendant, but my fingers felt numb.

The resemblance. Her emotion. Marcus's attachment to her. His need to hide her from me. Her necklace. I didn't understand what it all meant. But it had to mean *something*.

Uncounted minutes passed, a fire alarm went off, and people rushed into, around, and out of the room, scouring it of the blood and death and leaving behind the scent of bleach. It stung my nose, but still I stared at *La Donna Triste*. I needed to know who she was.

"Little Ivanov?" Marcus was standing on the other side of the sculpture. "Lex?"

I tore my eyes away from *La Donna*'s face to look up at him.

"Dom has a fresh dress for you." He pointed toward the doorway that led out to the rest of the museum's second floor with his chin. "You should go change so we can return to—"

"Who is she?" My fingertips were still touching the pendant hanging around my neck.

Marcus inhaled and exhaled seven times and stared down at me with guarded eyes, but he didn't say anything.

"*Who* is she, Marcus, and why does she look like *me*?" My old friend hysteria had finally shown up to the party, making my voice shriller than I liked.

Still, Marcus said nothing.

"At least tell me why you didn't want me to see her . . . why you were hiding this from me. Please, Marcus . . ."

His mouth opened and shut, and he winced. Wincing was bad. Wincing meant he was considering continuing to hide this mysterious truth from me because he thought dealing with whatever anger doing so would incur from me might be better than dealing with my reaction to the truth.

Closing my eyes, I took a deep breath, exhaling slowly. "I'll be with Dom. Let me know when you're ready to leave," I said as I stood, looking down at the floor, at the barren wall behind him, at Sara, who was being handcuffed by a Nejerette in the corner of the room, anywhere but at Marcus. I made my way to the doorway in a fog but paused before I reached it, turning my head just enough that I could see Marcus in my peripheral vision. "Giovanni?"

"Dazed, but alright. I knocked him out when it all started, to protect him."

"Good." I swallowed. "That's good." Sara's pettiness may have resulted in the deaths of a handful of Set cult followers, but at least the innocent young man was safe. I turned my head a fraction more, just enough that I could see Marcus's eyes; he was staring down at *La Donna Triste,* his face etched with longing.

Fissures spread through my heart, cracking it and causing little pieces to crumble away. This was the problem with loving Marcus; he could wound me so deeply with just a look.

"Lex?" Dom touched my shoulder. "Come on. Let's get you changed."

6

HER & ME

When Marcus opened the bedroom door, I was sitting on the foot of our bed; I had been for nearly an hour. He shut the door quietly before crossing the room to one of the tall, east-facing windows, clasping his hands behind his back as he stared down at the gardens. That he always chose that stance, preferred to look outside rather than at me whenever we were at odds, was incredibly frustrating. And even more frustrating was that I doubted his go-to reaction would ever change.

I waited, staring at his back. I waited for him to explain, to tell me something—anything—that would help me understand.

"Are you alright?" he finally asked.

My hands clenched, gripping the muted floral fabric of my second sundress of the day.

He showed me his profile, but his eyes remained downcast. "I know it bothers you . . . when I kill."

I snorted. That probably should have been what was bothering me, but it wasn't. I hadn't thought much about the bodies since I'd laid eyes on *her*.

"I had no choice, Lex," he continued. "I had to get them out of the way so I could—"

"Why does she look like me?"

When he still didn't answer, only returned to looking out the window, I stood, took several steps toward him, and gripped his shoulder. I pulled him around to face me. He could have resisted. To his credit, he didn't.

"Why does she look like me, Marcus?" I narrowed my eyes as I glared up at his perfect face. "Or is it that *I* look like *her*?" A fetid lump sprouted tendrils of dread in my stomach. "Is she someone you knew . . . someone you loved? Is my resemblance to her what drew you to me in the first place?" *Stop it,* I told myself. *Just shut up! Stop talking! You're being an idiot!* But I kept on going without a second's pause. "Is that why you didn't want me to see her—because you didn't want me to find out your secret?"

Marcus clenched his jaw, but still said nothing.

"Who was she? One of your human wives? One of the mothers of your children?" I growled in frustration and yanked on the falcon pendant, breaking the chain. "Did you give this to me because I reminded you of her?" I threw it at him. "Damn it, Marcus, just tell me, because thinking of all the possibilities, all of the reasons for more secrets—I can't . . ."

Cold washed over me in a wave, and my skin prickled with goose bumps. There was another option, something I was missing . . . ignoring. Something that was too far-fetched, too impossible, too terrifying. But it wasn't impossible, not really . . . not anymore.

"Nuin could travel through space *and* time," I said slowly, searching Marcus's eyes. "I have half of his power, and we already know I can jump from place to place, so I *could* be able to move through time, too . . . which would mean I could travel back centuries . . . and she really could be . . . me."

I stared into Marcus's eyes, waiting for a flash of recognition, for some sort of confirmation. Nothing, not even a raised eyebrow or a widened eye. No hint of surprise.

"You already knew. Of course you did." I laughed sardonically and crossed my arms over my chest. "You remember me being there, don't you. You remember me being a part of your life *five hundred years ago,* and you still didn't tell me about it."

"Not precisely."

I threw my hands up in the air. "Oh, well . . . enlighten me, please." I recrossed my arms.

"I dreamt her—you."

"You dreamt me."

Marcus looked up at the ceiling, clenching and unclenching his jaw several times. When he lowered his gaze, focusing on me, his eyes were alight with emotion. "The first time I saw you, when I was watching over you for Alexander, I recognized you. I had Vali send me a picture of *La Donna Triste* so I could compare you to her, write off the similarities I saw between the two of you as a flight of my overactive imagination." He shook his head. "But comparing you to her only confirmed what my heart already knew: that somehow, the two of you were one and the same."

"So why—"

Marcus silenced me with slight narrowing of his eyes. "Until a week ago, I thought it was an At-dream. My control over my ba is such that I don't have At-dreams often anymore, and when I do, it's only when the subject of the echo is integral to my future." The corner of his mouth curved upward. "Which seemed more and more logical the better I came to know you."

The ice coating my veins thawed a little. How could it not, when he was looking at me like that?

"But once you absorbed a full half of Nuin's power, I came to think that maybe, just maybe, you actually visited me in 1517 . . . and considering that Nuin could also conceal memories completely . . ."

My arms relaxed until they hung at my sides, and I shook my head, laughing softly. It was a humorless sound. The possibility that I would, at some point in my future, travel back five hundred years to visit Marcus's past was so unfathomable it was laughable. But that didn't make it any less *possible*.

"You figured I could've done the same to you, traveled back in time and blocked your memory of it."

"Precisely, Little Ivanov."

I frowned, far from mollified. "So, why didn't you just tell me?" My brow furrowed, and my eyes stung with a sudden welling of unshed tears. "Why'd you hide *La Donna* from me? Because that's why you didn't want me to come to the Accademia today, and why you left me in the gallery so you could go off with Giovanni alone . . ." I squeezed my eyes shut. "You didn't want me to see her, because you didn't want me to know the truth, and I need to know why, Marcus. I *need* to know why you felt the need to hide that from me."

He pressed his lips together.

I shook my head and cleared my throat. "I need to be alone . . . to think." Heading for the door, I said, "I'm going down to the gardens."

"Lex . . ."

I opened the door and stepped into the hallway, but I paused, giving him a chance to explain. He didn't.

"Please don't follow me," I said before shutting the door.

7

THOUGHT & REASON

The palazzo's gardens were both immaculate and varied. Manicured English gardens and terraced patches of lush grass and adorable herb and vegetable gardens all flowed into one another. There were small fountains and large fountains, some hidden by hedges or trees or stone walls, some out in the open, some filled with or surrounded by stone sculptures of people or animals or mythical creatures. There was even a tall hedge maze, and in the center, my favorite fountain of all—a small, plain, circular fountain surrounded by a low stone lip with a single pedestal in the center, gently spilling water back into the pool. I loved it because it was the most likely place to find solitude, and there were times when I wanted nothing more than to be alone.

The fountain was so hidden away, so burdensome to get to, and so unremarkable that it was one of the few places I'd never seen another person. Since absorbing half of Nuin's power, I'd been welcomed as an honorary member of the Council of Seven, filling Set's long-abandoned seat. And with my new position came a life that was more constricting than it had been back in the Heru Compound save for one thing: at the palazzo, I didn't have to let guards shadow me wherever I went. There were constant guards patrolling the perimeter of the grounds, not to mention the highest quality security systems and alarms.

I meandered around the bends in the hedge maze, listening to the chirping of tiny birds and the scurrying of critters within the manicured shrubbery. I wondered how long the hedge maze had been there, and if it was original to the grounds. The palazzo had been built by the Council in the fourteenth century, and considering that Nejerets weren't big embracers of change, instead preferring to hold onto their familiar, antiquated ways for as long as they could, I figured it was a distinct possibility.

Which led to another, more troublesome thought: *Have I been here before . . . hundreds of years ago?*

I reached the break in the hedge that opened to the fountain in the center of the maze. It wasn't a large space, with only several feet of paving stones surrounding the fountain in a geometric fan pattern, and the coziness only made it that much more perfect.

Toeing off my sandals, I stepped onto the sun-heated stones, welcoming their soothing warmth, and lowered myself to the ground to sit beside the fountain. Whether it was because the pose was fresh in my mind from obsessing over the sculpture for the past few hours or because it was simply a natural position for me, I found myself sitting exactly as *La Donna Triste* had been for the past five centuries.

Lazily, I trailed my fingertips in the crystal-clear water, watching the ripples spread across its surface until they converged with those caused by the trickle of falling water.

I heard footsteps on the gravel leading into the center of the maze, into my sanctuary. I would've noticed them when the intruder first entered the maze, had I been paying attention. But I'd been lost in a maze of my own making.

The footsteps stopped as the intruder stepped onto the paving stones, and I inhaled deeply. An enticingly familiar and painfully alluring spicy scent was barely detectable, but it was there. I should have known he would come.

"I told you not to follow me."

"I've never been good at following orders."

I narrowed my eyes at my own, wavy reflection. "You swore an oath to obey me."

"You rejected my oath."

I smiled, just a little.

With a soft plunk, a piece of gravel broke the water's surface and drifted down the several feet to the bottom of the pool.

"I am that pond, and you are that pebble."

Raising my eyebrows, I glanced at him over my shoulder. "Some girls get compared to flowers or butterflies, but not me. I'm a tiny rock."

The corners of Marcus's mouth curved upward the barest amount. "When you came into my life five centuries ago, you must also have been like that pebble. You caused ripples, and though they eventually died away, the pebble remained." He stepped to the edge of the fountain, the side of his shoe just a few inches from my hand, and crouched down. The fine fabric of his slacks brushed against the back of my arm, and I shivered. "The essence of your being resonates with me so deeply that it was impossible for you to block my memory of you completely." He placed his fingertips under my chin and turned my head toward him, tilting my face upward. "You changed me, and you couldn't lock that away."

I stared into his liquid gold eyes, my unshed tears from earlier finally escaping. "Tell me why you hid it from me."

Marcus raised his hand higher and wiped away a tear as it glided down my cheek. "This." He looked into my eyes like he was searching my soul. "I didn't want to upset you."

My blood heated, and I had to hold back the urge to scream at him. I shifted, curling my legs under me and turning so I was kneeling, facing him and glaring for all I was worth. "But don't you see, Marcus? It's not the possibility that I'll travel back in time that's so upsetting—it's that you don't think I can handle *knowing* I'll travel back in time." My hands balled into fists, and I howled in frustration. "God, sometimes you make me so mad, I just want to—"

"Hit me?" Marcus arched an eyebrow. "You've done it before, Little Ivanov; why hold back now?"

Gritting my teeth, I raised my fists, opened my hands, and splayed my fingers in the air until my hands shook. Before I could give in and actually hit him—which would do no good, considering his muscles were so well-honed he was practically made of stone himself—I pushed off the ground and strode away several steps.

"You're insufferable, and infuriating, and"—I turned, pointing at him, and he froze in the middle of rising—"do *not* get up, Marcus."

For once, he listened to me and eased himself back down, sitting fully on the paving stones. He extended one leg in front of him and bent the other, propping his arm on his knee. Wearing his fresh white dress shirt, pewter-gray slacks, and Italian leather shoes, he looked like he was posing for a high-fashion photo shoot. The observation only angered me further.

I started pacing on the opposite side of the fountain. "You were right not to compare me to a flower or a butterfly, I'll give you that, but do you know why?" I didn't wait for him to answer. "Because I'm not some fragile, delicate thing. I'm not going to break if you push me too far. I mean, I've been shot in the stomach, I've watched you die *thousands* of times, my God damn father is a psychotic megalomaniac hell-bent on either controlling the world or destroying it, *and* I currently contain half of the power of the strongest Nejeret who ever lived . . ." *. . . and in another timeline, I killed Set and watched you die,* really *die,* I didn't say.

I stopped pacing and glared across the fountain, placing my

hands on my hips. "Not you and not all the hard truth in the world is going to break me, so just—damn it, Marcus, just stop trying to protect me from the truth. Stop holding back. I can handle it." My hands slipped from my hips to hang limply at my sides. "I can handle it."

8

TWO & ONE

Marcus watched me with an unreadable expression for dozens of heartbeats, tens of shaky breaths, an eternity of say-somethings.

I swallowed roughly as I held his gaze, refusing to look away . . . refusing to show weakness.

"Are you finished?" His tone was cool, controlled; it was his on-the-brink-of-snapping tone, which always gave me shivers.

I swallowed again and nodded.

Very slowly, Marcus rose until he was standing at full height. He started prowling toward me around the edge of the fountain.

I took a step backward.

"My delicate little butterfly . . ." Colder. More controlled.

I backed away another step.

He sneered haughtily. "My precious little flower . . ." Ice and steel.

I glanced behind me, looking for the gap in the hedge, seriously considering fleeing. It was a purely instinctive predator-prey reaction. I knew he wouldn't hurt me, not really, but I still never felt completely comfortable around Marcus when he was like this—unpredictable and domineering and absolutely, completely in control of everything.

I started to turn, started to take a step toward the opening.

"Stop," he said, and I did.

I scanned the tall hedge, trying to come up with some way to diffuse him, to take back some of the control.

"Those are things I might have called other women," he said. "Other lovers." His words stung worse than a slap in the face. He knew that one of my weakest points was my jealousy of the hundreds, maybe even thousands of women he'd been intimately involved with over his long life, and he was prodding me —goading me—on purpose.

I narrowed my eyes.

"But never you, Little Ivanov. I would never call you either of those things."

As he took a few final steps, closing the distance between us, he reached his hand into his right pocket. I glanced down as he removed the lapis lazuli falcon pendant, broken chain and all. "You are the only woman I would ever call my she-falcon . . . the only woman I would ask to wear my symbol . . . the only woman who makes me feel like I don't have to hold back . . ."

I stood as still as *La Donna Triste* as Marcus held the necklace up, knotting the broken chain behind my neck so the falcon pendant once again rested against my breastbone.

"You are the only woman who's ever made me feel like I've been set free." He ran his fingertips ever so lightly up and down my neck. "And if I try to protect you from hard truths"—his fingertips traveled lower, moving over the bare skin on my shoulders—"it's only because I'm selfish." He hooked his thumbs under the thin straps of my sundress and pulled them over the curves of my shoulders. "It pains me to see you upset, and I don't like to be pained."

I sucked in a breath as he started unfastening the tiny

buttons running the length of the front of my dress. My heart galloped.

"I try to protect you because I love you, not because I'm holding back . . . never because I'm holding back. Not with you."

A flush spread over my skin as Marcus undid enough buttons that the top half of my dress slipped down, baring me from the waist up. My thin, lacy bra was the only thing keeping me even partially decent. "Marcus . . ." I crossed my arms over my chest protectively and glanced over my shoulder toward the opening in the hedge. "What are you doing?"

"I need you to feel how much I love you, Lex." He slid his hands around me, finding and unclasping my bra within seconds. As he guided its straps over my shoulders and down my arms, he pulled my forearms away from my chest. "I need you to feel it . . . to understand. I *need* you to understand . . ."

His lips were suddenly on mine, silken and feverish and greedy, and his hands were behind my head, tangled in my loose waves, running down my back, hitching up my skirt. His need—his desire—was so intense, it acted like lighter fluid on my own, and heat blossomed low in my abdomen.

Yes, I realized, *this is what I need, to feel how much he loves me . . . to feel* him.

My fingers found his belt buckle as he pushed down my underwear, and I had it unfastened by the time I was kicking the lacy fabric away. Marcus broke our kiss, and gasping for breath, I looked down as he knocked my hands away. With a soft grunt, he opened the front of his trousers so roughly that the top button popped off. He shoved his pants down, freeing himself as he dropped to his knees and pulled me down onto his lap.

We both groaned as he sank home, filling me completely, almost too much. With a hiss of pleasure, I rocked against him, savoring the feast of sensations—his hands gripping my hips, his breath hot against my neck. Him, inside me.

His fingers clenched, holding my hips in place, and he pulled his head back so he was gazing into my eyes. "Close your eyes," he whispered. "Don't see." Ever so slowly, achingly so, he lifted me then lowered me back down. "Don't hear." He repeated the deliberate motion. "Don't smell and don't taste." Again. "Just feel, my Lex. Just *feel*."

A hoarse sound that was part laugh, part groan rose from my chest, and I grasped onto Marcus's shoulders, feeling the hard muscles bunching as he continued to move my hips, gradually increasing the pace. I focused on nothing but him, nothing but the sensation of being joined to him . . . the mounting pleasure . . . the burgeoning ache . . . the devastating amount of unbridled love.

His breaths were coming faster, harder, as were mine. "Do you feel it? Do you feel how much I love you?"

And I *could*. His love for me was a tangible thing, a cord stretching between our hearts, resonating with the intensity of my own feelings for him. And it thickened, strengthened, solidified as our souls merged, making our bond even more unbreakable. He was inside me, not just physically; his ba was intertwining with mine, making us, for a few glorious minutes, a single, unified entity.

"I feel it," I breathed. "Oh God, Marcus . . . I feel you. I *feel* you . . . your ba . . . oh God . . ." My fingers dug into his shoulders as my pleasure swelled.

"Yes," Marcus hissed, and there was no more talking. There was only a brief eternity of ecstasy as we relished being truly joined.

9

FUTURE & PAST

"I think we missed our meeting with the realtor . . ." I tapped my toes against the surface of the water in a haphazard, staccato rhythm. I was sitting at the very edge of the pond, my knees drawn up to my bare chest and my arms wrapped around my thighs. Marcus was sprawled on his side behind me, still wearing all of his clothes, tracing hieroglyphs on my back with his fingertips.

He chuckled, the sound low and silken, going a long way in recharging my spent desire. "We can reschedule."

"For tomorrow?" I craned my neck to look back at him.

He shook his head, his golden tiger eyes filled with apology. "It's too dangerous right now, Little Ivanov. I wish . . ." Sighing, he shook his head again. "It doesn't matter. It's just too dangerous right now."

I offered him a small smile. "It's okay. I understand." Looking back at the fountain, I watched the water ripple around my toes. "Does it bother you that you can't remember me . . . from before?"

I heard the rustle of clothing, then felt the press of soft lips against my shoulder. "No."

"Why not?"

"Because it hasn't happened yet . . . for you. I'm still holding out hope that, one day, you'll unblock my mind, and I *will* remember."

Thanks for reading! You've reached the end of Resonance, *but Lex's adventures continue in* Time Anomaly (Echo Trilogy, #2).

DISSONANCE

1

HOPES & FEARS

"I'll be right back," I called through Denny Hall's closing glass door and hurried down the steep stairs on my way to get coffee, careful not to slip. I hugged myself to fend off the damp chill as I made my way along the slick paved pathway. I was antsy and fidgety, so much so that I'd completely forgotten to retrieve my jacket before rushing outside, and a brisk walk through the seemingly constant Seattle drizzle would do my frayed nerves good.

It had just been a nightmare—or daymare, *I told myself. It had all been in my head. But I couldn't help stopping on the sidewalk by the scene of the imaginary crime and staring down at the spot on the asphalt where Dr. Ramirez's lifeless body had lain what felt like only moments ago.*

I blinked, squeezing my eyelids shut in an attempt to block out a memory from a dream that had felt far too real. When I opened my eyes again, my heartbeat tripped over itself, and I screamed, "NO!"

Dr. Ramirez was there. He shouldn't have been; I'd just left him in the lobby of Denny Hall. He was supposed to be inside the old building, safe and sound and not here. *Not in danger. This couldn't be happening.*

He'd just stepped onto the street and was jogging across. At hearing my shout, he paused to look back at me, and not a second later, a speeding station wagon slammed into him.

Dr. Ramirez's body rolled up onto the hood, his head hitting the windshield with a sickening crack before he slid back down and was dumped on the asphalt. His arm flopped out to the side, landing in a grimy puddle.

"Oh my God! Dr. Ramirez!" I stumbled across the sidewalk and onto the university's main drag. But I already knew it was too late. I already knew, because I'd dreamed about almost this exact, horrific thing happening mere minutes ago.

I already knew that Dr. Ramirez was dead.

"BUT THERE ARE NO GUARANTEES, MESWETT." DR. Julian Sands, veterinarian to the Nejeret stars, stared down at Rus, the tiny, still-as-stone kitten curled up in near-eternal slumber beside Marcus's ancient little girl, Tarset. Both were frozen in time, appearing to be statues carved from quartz—Tarset, to prevent her body from giving in to the effects of a lethal poison, and Rus, because it was the only way to bring him with me into the future. "Not in cases like this," Dr. Sands continued, "because, well, there aren't any other cases like this."

"I see." I crossed my arms and cleared my throat. Disturbed as I'd been all morning by the third recurrence of the unsettling dream about my former graduate advisor being hit by a car—it was a near-exact replay of the first echo I'd ever witnessed, though thankfully it had never truly come to pass—I'd managed to pay attention to the highly esteemed and even more highly recommended vet pretty damn well.

Dr. Sands reached across the corner of the bed of solidified At and touched my shoulder. I made a small, unobtrusive hand gesture by my thigh—a preemptive attempt to keep Nik from taking offence at what he would no doubt perceive as an inappropriate and potentially threatening touch. I caught only the slightest movement from him in my periphery, but his heavy exhale told me he wasn't pleased that Dr. Sand's hand was on my shoulder.

Sometimes Nik could be so overprotective that he made Marcus's efforts to keep me safe look negligent in comparison. Considering my current *delicate* condition—that I was carrying unborn twins who were fated to restore balance to the universe, otherwise known as ma'at to the Nejerets' godlier ancestors, and that I was almost constantly on the verge of having a full-on freak-out breakdown worthy of my very own padded room because of said current condition—I didn't mind so much.

"I'm not suggesting we don't move forward with little Rus's transition," Dr. Sands said, "I'm just saying we should proceed with extreme caution . . . take it slow. Pathogens are tricky, and they evolve quickly—it would be impossible to predict what will and won't harm him. Any immunity he's developed so far will be irrelevant. He'll have to start over from scratch."

I swallowed, and it sounded obscenely loud in the barren, sterile room. Again, I said, "I see."

We were underground, in the basement of the main house in the Heru compound, in a small room on the periphery of Neffe's intricate home-lab setup, where she and Aset were leading up a team hard at work trying to find a solution to the Tarset problem—how to revive a little girl who'd been poisoned thousands of years ago and frozen in time ever since. Tarset and Rus had been down in this room since we'd returned from the Nejeret Oasis in the Sahara a week earlier. It was a cold space, hardly ideal for a child, and we were all eager to restore Marcus's little girl—and me my ten-week-going-on-five-thousand-year-old kitten—to life as soon as possible. Or, rather, as soon as was safe.

Dr. Sands was renowned throughout the Nejeret community for being the most experienced and knowledgeable practitioner of animal medicine alive today. He had over a millennium of caring for Nejeret pets under his belt, and he'd traveled halfway across the world to Bainbridge Island to help me with my tiny, out-of-time kitten situation. If anyone would be able to help Rus survive the transition into the modern world, it was this man.

Dr. Sands withdrew his hand from my shoulder and ran his fingers through his dirty blond hair. "Give me a couple days to draw up a plan and put together a full series of vaccinations, Meswett." He flashed me a brilliant smile, belying the mild uncertainty in his eyes. "I'm confident we'll have little Rus running around and bothering Thora in no time."

At the thought of Rus catting around with my older tabby, Thora, I actually managed to return the veterinarian's smile. I nodded and held my arm out toward the open doorway, where Nik and Dominic stood sentry and Carlisle, Marcus's "man," waited with his ever-present smartphone in hand. "Please, make yourself at home in the lab. Neffe won't mind."

Dominic snorted.

"Much," I added. "And just let Carlisle know what you need, and he'll help make the arrangements."

"Wonderful," Dr. Sands said. He started toward Carlisle and the guarded doorway to the lab, but he paused midway and looked at me over his shoulder. "It will be the same for the girl, you know . . . the adjustment to modern pathogens."

With a slow blink, I redirected my focus to Tarset's opalescent cherubic face and felt a single tear sneak over the brim of my eyelid and glide down my cheek. Tarset had been poisoned over five thousand years ago, and not only did we not know *what* Apep-Ankhesenpepi had used to poison the Oasis's water supply, we didn't even know if an antidote could be created or if the damage the poison had caused to Tarset's young body could be reversed. Her suspended state was the only thing keeping her from death. Once we unfroze her, the ancient little girl would be lucky if she survived long enough to worry about modern pathogens. Which was precisely why Neffe had hunted down the best and brightest scientifically minded Nejerets to assist her and Aset in finding a way to save Marcus's little girl.

"That's the least of her problems," I said quietly.

"Aren't you finished with your consult yet?" Neffe said, brusque as ever. I turned in time to see her brushing past Carlisle and Dr. Sands on her way into the room, what appeared to be a small insulated lunchbox slung over her shoulder. "My team can't do anything more until we have our samples." She strode toward me, stopped beside the At bed, and set the insulated container down next to Rus, then met my eyes and winked. "Which means I need your help right now, Nik, so I can get my samples."

I suppressed a grin. For whatever reason, Neffe loved being a pain in ass. It had taken me a while to pick up on it, but once it became obvious to Neffe that I was on to her, she started to find little ways to let me in on the joke. So far as I could tell, she simply liked to see how far she could push people. Probably because she was bored. Living for several millennia tended to do that to a person.

Nik let out a heavy sigh. "I just don't know if I'm up to it today." Due to his unusual circumstances of birth—being born of two Nejerets—Nik had his own minor sheut that, much like the borrowed sheut I'd been carrying for the past couple months, gave him certain powers beyond the normal Nejeret. In Nik's case, he could manipulate the very fabric of the At, giving it physical form or, as Neffe needed him to do, reverting At particles to their original molecular structure—Nejeret flesh and bone.

I glanced at Nik, taking in his bored expression, his usual hint of a smirk, but I didn't miss the sparkle of amusement in his too-pale blue eyes. My attention returned to Neffe just in time to catch the tail end of what appeared to be a rather pleased grin.

Carlisle escorted a somewhat confused Dr. Sands out of the room, leaving Nik, Dominic, Neffe, and myself behind.

"If you do not do what she wants, she'll go out of her way to make your life difficult until you give in," Dominic said, his French accent making the words sound like even more of a warning. "Trust me, I know."

Neffe gave me a look that said, "Yeah, he's probably right," as well as words ever could.

With a sigh, Nik pushed away from the wall and made his way to the bedside, feet dragging just a bit. "My sheut is at your disposal, *princess*."

Neffe closed her eyes for a moment, collecting herself. True, she liked acting the haughty, irritable vixen for fun, but she genuinely had a quicksilver disposition, and Nik's new favorite nickname for her—princess—was one of her triggers. It didn't matter that she'd grown up a princess in Middle Kingdom Egypt, the daughter of Queen Hatshepsut, or that her father had been the Nejeret equivalent to a king but had abdicated the figurative throne during Neffe's adolescence. She *hated* being called "princess."

"If you call me that one more time," Neffe said through clenched teeth, "I will tear that ridiculous ring out of your eyebrow."

Nik leaned in close to Neffe and whispered, "Promise?"

I could practically see the shiver work its way over her body, could all but sense her sudden discomfort as she sidled closer to me. Nik had that effect on people—whether it was the array of tattoos covering his body from the neck down in various shades of fading gray, his standoffish attitude, or the fact that Re, the godly being who'd once been the father of our kind, resided within his body, most people found him disturbing, Nejeret and human alike. Me? I just liked to think of him as *unique*.

Nik tossed me a shit-eating grin. He knew the effect he had on Neffe and pretty much everyone else. He *liked* it.

"So, um . . ." I looked from Nik to Neffe and back. "Should we get started? I know Marcus wanted to catch the ten o'clock ferry, and it's got to be nearly nine . . ."

"It's a quarter till," Dominic offered. I glanced at him, still standing sentry by the doorway, and offered him a small smile and a nod.

"Yes, yes, very well." Neffe pointed to Tarset's arm, shrouded in a thin but impervious and unmovable blanket. "Nik, I need you to restore her elbow area, maybe an inch above and an inch below. Then her mouth, just for a moment. That will give me blood, tissue, and saliva samples," she said, ticking each off on her fingers. "Which will have to be good enough. We can't risk restoring her vital organs, not even for a second, so *be careful*."

Surprised by the sudden heat in her voice, I glanced at Neffe's face. Her caramel eyes burned with an intensity I'd only seen a time or two before. And then it struck me—this wasn't just some little girl we were trying to revive, this was her sister. Though Neffe had never actually met Tarset, having been born over a thousand years later, they *were* sisters. I hadn't met any of Marcus's other children in modern times. Honestly, I wasn't sure if there were any others still living; his past families were a touchy subject for Marcus, and though I'd unearthed a fair bit of his humanity under the stony wall built up by millennia of life and death and love and loss, I still had a colossal amount of chiseling to do. In some ways, Marcus was almost as ensconced in time as little Tarset.

When Nik didn't respond to Neffe's cautioning to take care, Neffe made to reach for his arm, but stopped herself short. Instead, she made a fist. "If you're at all unsure . . ."

"Nik is not entirely confident in his ability to wield his sheut so specifically." The words had been uttered using Nik's vocal chords, tongue, and lips, but their cadence and accent hinted at another speaker entirely. One quick glance at Nik's face, at the open, relaxed expression and the opalescent irises now staring back at me, confirmed it—Nik was no longer in control; Re was. "I will do this for you instead, Neferure." His lips curved upwards in a smile that looked nothing like Nik's. "Personally, I'd rather not feel the pain of this ring tearing through our flesh."

"I—I—" Neffe stammered. "Of—of course not, Great Father." She cleared her throat. "I wouldn't have actually . . . I mean, I—"

"It is fine, child," Re-Nik said, touching Neffe's arm. "I understand more than you think. Now, shall we begin?"

2

WANTING & WAITING

"I am *so* excited," Kat said, bouncing on the balls of her feet as she stood at the bottom of the grand stairway in the main house—what I'd come to call simply "the house." It was easily a mansion, and as classically designed as it was on the outside, it was equally modern and subdued on the inside. And the thing was enormous, boasting at least a dozen bedrooms and enough secondary rooms to complete a small neighborhood.

Watching my youngest—that I knew of—sister from one of several understated gray couches in the sitting room beside the entryway, I smiled to myself. In her cut-off jean shorts and flowy T-shirt, and with her hair coiled up in a messy topknot and the worn leather satchel containing her sketching supplies that seemed to be on her at all times lately hanging easily across her body, she looked the stereotypical eighteen-year-old. She *looked* carefree and confident, not a worry in the world. My smile wilted. That couldn't be further from the truth.

"I think we're all ready to get out and stretch our legs somewhere that isn't *here*," I said, interrupting my souring mood by filling the silence. ". . . and isn't packed full of Nejerets." I glanced at Neffe, who was seated on the opposite end of the couch from me, flipping through a scientific journal like she was skimming for the season's latest and greatest in a fashion magazine. "I meant no offense, of course, it's just . . ." We'd been cooped up in the compound for the past week, and I was fairly certain we were all starting to feel like caged animals.

"Trust me, Lex, I get it." Neffe offered me a minute smile without actually looking at me. "I'm as eager as young Kat for our little trip into the city." As was I, though after the dream I'd woken from again this morning, I wagered I had very different reasons than the others. More than anything, I needed to reassure myself that the recurring nightmare had been only that: a mere figment of an overwrought mind's overactive imagination.

I returned my attention to Kat, taking note of her suddenly stiff posture and how her hands balled into fists at her sides. She took a deep breath. Then another. And I waited for the impending explosion. She could stand Neffe calling her "young Kat" less than Neffe could stand Nik's nickname of "princess."

Kat took one more, deeper breath, and I was in the middle of mentally commending her for her unusual show of self-restraint when she opened her mouth and yelled "*Marcus!*" up the stairs. Very, very loudly. My ears rang from the unexpected influx of way too much sound. Sometimes heightened Nejeret senses could be a real pain.

"Okay!" I jumped up and rushed to the stairway. "Let's not do that again . . . ever, hmm?"

Kat turned to me as I approached, her expression sheepish. "Sorry."

I touched her shoulder as I passed her and headed up the stairs. "I'm going to check on Marcus. I'm sure he's getting ready right now." He'd better be, if we wanted to make the ferry. Ascending the final few stairs, I glanced back at Kat. "Go track down Dom and Nik, will you? Let them know we're about to head out."

"Yeah, okay." And just like that, she was back to bouncing as she skipped along the hallway that led to the other rooms deeper in the house.

"Thank you for not leaving me alone with her," I heard Neffe say under her breath, just loud enough for me to hear.

I rolled my eyes. *Family* . . .

I STARED DOWN AT THE SPARKLING RIPPLES OF WATER from the upper deck of the ferry, seeing another time, another place in the Puget Sound's inky depths. In my mind, I was surrounded by jagged limestone outcroppings and sand and the driest heat I'd ever felt. Before me, Marcus—or, rather, Heru—knelt on the rock-strewn sand, a tall wall of limestone on one side of us, a pile of boulders on the other. My memory of him staring up at me while he pledged his life to mine was so fresh in my mind it might as well have happened mere hours ago, not thousands of *years* ago.

I shook my head and frowned, embracing the refreshing sea air. It was a perfect August day in the Sound—a solid eighty degrees, ideal tank-top-and-sandals weather. Ideal ferry weather.

"My father would have enjoyed the ferry ride greatly today," Neffe said from beside me. She'd been my silent companion at the deck railing for some fifteen minutes, and I'd utilized that time to thoroughly lose myself in thought.

"Mm-hmm." Thinking of Marcus—or, more specifically, of his absence—I suppressed another frown.

"Whatever the Council of Seven was discussing must have been very important for him to miss this," Neffe added, and I glanced at her, just long enough to see the concern in her eyes. I'd fought hard to keep our little day trip alive once it became clear that Marcus wouldn't be able to leave his virtual meeting with the Council for hours yet, and Neffe had been my main ally, but I hadn't expected Marcus to actually agree. As silly as it sounds, considering I'd gotten my way, I felt a little let down.

"It was important," I said. "—ish." I caught a glimpse of Nik out of the corner of my eye; he was leaning against the railing several dozen feet up deck from us, his back to the water as he kept a close eye on everyone and everything within his range of sight. Marcus and the Council had been discussing him, specifically whether or not they should force him to be the ninth member of the Council of Seven, what with me being the honorary eighth member and the Council having a hard time making any decisions now that they boasted an even number of members. Remotely, I wondered if they'd be changing the name now that the "of Seven" no longer applied.

Marcus had called for a short break when I'd come upstairs to check on him, but not before I'd heard the heated voices coming from the conference room.

"I can't leave right now, Little Ivanov," Marcus told me, regret filling his burnished golden eyes. "We'll have to postpone until tomorrow."

I pressed my lips together and studied his resigned features. "Are you sure you have to be here for this?" I asked, flicking my eyes toward the shut door behind him and the conference room with its six monitors, one for each of the members of the Council of Seven. I'd ducked out of the meeting when Dr. Sands had arrived a couple hours earlier, and it had been little more than a silent standoff when I'd been present. The discussion was pointless, which I'd already expressed . . . thus the silent standoff. But none of them knew Nik—or Re—as well as I did, not even Marcus. I'd tried to tell them that nobody could make Nik do something he didn't want to do, especially not when Re himself had no interest in taking part in the Nejeret governing body, but several of the Council members had refused to believe me. Surely Marcus's time was better spent elsewhere . . . like in Seattle with me.

Marcus reached out and curved his hand around the side of my neck, brushing his thumb slowly over my lips until they parted. He made a low, guttural sound, something between a groan and a sigh. "Much as I hate to see such disappointment in your eyes, Little Ivanov, yes, I need to be here for this."

Grasping his wrist, I turned my face to the side and kissed his palm. Meeting his eyes, I pulled back a hairsbreadth and said, "But I *don't."*

I watched Marcus's striking features tense. "Lex . . ."

I stood a little taller. "There's no reason I shouldn't go without you." Before he could protest, I barreled on without thought. "We've had zero indication that anyone has any interest in hurting me right now, and *Saga and Heimdall already scoured the stable portions of the At and saw* nothing *to be worried about in Seattle today. Besides, Dr. Ramirez rearranged his entire schedule today to fit me in." Apparently he had an artifact for me to look at, though I had no idea what it was or where he'd come by it, just that it had made him think of me. His email a few days back had sparked unexpected happiness, as though he was my last true connection to the purely human world, and now with the dreams about him dying, I was especially determined to visit him today.*

"Plus," Neffe said from behind me, "both Nik and Dom will be there, and even you've all but admitted that Nik is better at protecting Lex than you are." I sucked in my breath and leaned back a little as soon as the words were out of Neffe's mouth. That had been the absolutely wrong thing for her—for anyone—to say to Marcus.

My bond-mate withdrew his hand and clenched it into a fist, and my whole body tensed in anticipation of what I was betting would be a rather grand argument. Marcus closed his eyes, took a deep breath, and slowly released it, then relaxed his hand and looked at me. "Very well, Little Ivanov, if you still wish to go into the city today, you have my—"

My eyes narrowed in anticipation of the next word that would come out of his mouth, and he paused. So help me, if he even started to utter the word "permission" . . .

Marcus's perfect, chiseled cheek twitched. "You have my blessing."

I flashed him a humorless smile. Clearly we were still working some of the kinks out of our relationship.

"YES, WELL, MY FATHER CAN SPEND ALL DAY IN HIS precious meeting for all I care." Neffe nudged my shoulder. "At least we get to get out and have some fun, yeah?"

I met her gaze and smiled, knowing full well it didn't touch my eyes. I felt off, and not only because Marcus hadn't been able to join us. No, it was something else. Something different. It was as though I was waiting for something to happen; I just didn't know *what* I was waiting for. *It's probably just the dream,* I told myself.

Neffe touched her fingertips to my forearm. "I'm going to run in and grab a coffee. Do you want anything?"

I shook my head. "Thanks, though," I said absently, and she walked away. In my periphery, I spotted Kat approaching from the stern, her sketchbook hugged to her chest. Her expression darkened suddenly, and she made an about-face and headed instead toward the bench where Dominic was sitting. Turning to confirm my suspicion of what she'd seen, I leaned my hip against the railing, not the least bit surprised to find that Nik had moved closer. His back was still to the water, but he now stood right beside me.

I crossed my arms over my chest and narrowed my eyes. "You know, you have the most interesting effect on people."

He glanced at me sidelong, his pale eyes glittering. "I hadn't noticed."

I rolled my eyes. "I'm sure."

"I'm not the only one who has an *interesting* effect on people, you know." Nik turned his face to me, his usual smirk absent for once.

"What are you—" My eyes widened. "You mean *me*?" I said, touching the tip of my index finger to my chest.

Nik tucked his hands into his jeans pockets—they were a dark gray instead of his usual black, his concession to the warm weather—and shrugged one shoulder. His gaze grew distant, and he nodded slowly. "You know, when I first met you in that temple back in Men-Nefer, I thought it was the sheut you carried, but then when I sat with you on the bus, more or less sheut-free, well . . . that blew *that* theory all to hell. I was actually a little nervous to talk to you." He laughed to himself. "I mean, even with just a sliver of Re's sheut, you were still the most intimidating person I'd ever met—other than the Great Father, of course."

"Of course," I said dryly, mostly because I was too caught off guard say anything else. *I* was intimidating? Like, Nik-level intimidating? I turned back toward the water and leaned my forearms on the railing.

And still underneath the confusion at Nik's revelation, I felt it: that oh-so-strange sense of waiting.

3

WAS & IS

Dominic drove the Range Rover off the ferry, Neffe in the front passenger seat, Nik and me right behind them, and Kat in the very back, earbuds in and iPod blaring something with equal amounts of whininess and yelling and that was downright terrible. I was eternally grateful for headphones, especially where Kat's music was concerned. I just wished I could turn down my heightened sense of hearing so I wouldn't be able to hear the ear-sore *at all*.

And then there was Neffe, who'd taken control of the SUV's stereo system and was continuing her mission to convert us all into smooth jazz enthusiasts. It wasn't that I disliked her taste in music; rather, it just sort of faded into the background whenever I was listening to it. When Nik started humming along, I glanced at him, surprised that he was familiar enough with the tune to harmonize with it perfectly. But he didn't notice, just kept on staring out the window and humming softly.

Some twenty minutes later, we were exiting I-5 and making our way down Forty-Fifth Street toward the north end of the University of Washington campus. I stirred out of my car coma when Dominic continued straight through an intersection instead of turning right and heading toward the hospital, where Neffe would be spending the afternoon in the better-equipped labs running tests on Tarset's blood, tissue, and saliva samples.

Money, I was quickly learning, could buy almost anything, including access to world-renowned research facilities via an exorbitant donation. And if there was one thing Heru's line wasn't lacking in, it was money. Being able to see the future and all that . . . But it was the doors that money could open that might just prove invaluable. Neffe would be using this expensive opportunity to compare her samples to what Aset claimed was one of the most extensive libraries of poisons, toxins, and pathogens we were likely to find outside of a CDC facility.

I leaned forward and placed my hand on the top of Dominic's seat. "Where are you going?"

"To the lot behind Denny."

"But why? Then Neffe'll be wasting a solid forty minutes walking to and from the hospital, and she could use that time in the labs." I shook my head. "All I'm doing is meeting with Dr. Ramirez, and that's not for another hour. At least drop her off first."

"I don't mind the walk," Neffe said. "I prefer it, actually. It helps me process my findings."

"*And* this is the best way to minimize your exposure to danger." Dominic's eyes met mine in the rearview mirror for the briefest moment. "Which is my main priority, considering your condition."

"That's ridiculous," I snapped. "I'm pregnant, Dom, I'm not an invalid." But even as I said the words, I knew that to the other four Nejerets in the car, an invalid was exactly what I was. The nearly impossible physiological phenomenon that had allowed a Nejerette like myself to even become pregnant muted my body's natural ability to regenerate, making me as vulnerable as a regular ol' human. This didn't seem nearly as worrisome to me as it did to them; after all, I'd spent two and a half decades as a vulnerable human and barely half a year as a Nejerette. The others' silence following my hasty protestation only confirmed what I was just now coming to accept weeks into the pregnancy. For the next eight months, I'd be weakened, fragile, vulnerable—an invalid. Damn it.

Instead of arguing, I crossed my arms over my chest, stared out the window, and kept my mouth shut as Dominic parked in the small lot behind Denny Hall. The century-old anthropology building was stunning as ever, with its chateau-like exterior, proud bell tower, and windows gleaming with reflected sunlight. I wasn't the least bit surprised that being back here felt a lot like coming home. Even if I was a tad bit irritated.

Neffe hopped out almost as soon as we came to a stop, not even waiting for Dominic to turn off the engine. "I'll text you when I'm on my way back," she told Dominic, then started to shut the door.

My half-brother reached across the center console and stopped the door from shutting completely with a palm on the side panel. "Perhaps it would be wise to take Katarina with you." I glanced back, not the least bit surprised to find Kat staring out the window, apparently oblivious to the conversation . . . or to the fact that we'd even parked. "She could assist your work."

"She would only get in my way," Neffe said. "Besides, I'm sure she'd much prefer to stay with you and Lex and . . ." She cleared her throat. "With you and Lex."

I watched Kat in my peripheral vision. She gave no indication that she'd heard, which wasn't surprising considering that her earbuds were still in place. Except I could no longer hear her music. Which meant that earbuds or no, she could definitely hear Dominic's and Neffe's mutual attempts to pawn her off on the other.

My heart twanged with sympathy and more than a hint of empathy. I was no stranger to feeling like an unwelcome burden, either; after all, Marcus had run far and fast and had stayed away for months as soon as he'd figured out who I really was. I couldn't stand the idea of Kat feeling unwanted all day, not when today was supposed to be our one outing for who knew how long. Not at all.

"Good!" I said, hoping the single word hadn't sounded over-enthusiastic. "This'll give me a chance to show her all my old haunts . . . maybe convert her into a future Husky." I didn't miss the way Nik's eyes narrowed the slightest bit, the way the corner of his mouth tensed, like he was holding back a frown, or maybe a smile.

"How lovely," Neffe said. "Can I go now? I do have a lot to do in a short period of time . . ."

In one smooth motion, Dominic let go of the door and straightened in his seat. Just as quickly, Neffe shut the door and was walking away from the car.

I twisted in my seat and patted Kat's knee. "Ready, Freddie?"

She made a show of pulling out her headphones as she turned red-rimmed, glassy eyes my way. She averted her gaze down to her phone almost immediately. Oh yeah, she'd definitely heard everything.

Kat and I had to wait a solid ten minutes for Dominic and Nik to scout the area immediately surrounding Denny Hall. Kat moved up to Nik's middle seat instead of waiting in the back.

We were silent for several minutes, her phone forgotten in her hand and her eyes locked on the seemingly abandoned campus just beyond the window while I stared out at the small patch of road that had played so prominently in the dream. Physically being here, so close to the spot where I'd seen Dr. Ramirez die—real or not—was proving to be even more unsettling than the dream itself had been.

Gone was the brief blip of comfort I felt at returning to this place. Now, I felt antsy and on edge. I felt like I should've stayed with Marcus on Bainbridge, like I shouldn't have been here.

Must be the hormones, I thought, shaking my head. Likely, they were to blame for all of it—the weird feeling, the dream, my irritation with Marcus for agreeing to let me go . . .

Finally, Kat cleared her throat. "Thanks," she said quietly. When I turned my head to look at her, I found her still staring out the window.

I studied her profile, not for the first time searching for the similarities between us that others claimed were so obvious when they saw us together. I supposed it wasn't surprising; we were half-sisters through Set, after all, though I still had a hard time seeing the resemblance with either Kat or my other known half-sibling, Dominic. I figured it was psychological—I'd met both of them thinking they were strangers, unrelated to me in any way. I couldn't have been more wrong.

"Thanks for what?" I asked, smiling to myself. I was *glad* I'd been so wrong, because I adored both of these strangers-turned-siblings more than I ever could have imagined.

"Just, you know . . ." Kat shrugged and shifted in her seat, clearly uncomfortable. "For, like—I don't know." She wiped her hands on her cutoffs and looked at me for the first time since moving up a seat. The usual luster in her eyes was dimmed, her whole spunky demeanor somehow wilted. Even her crown of a bun seemed a little droopy.

"Hey." I reached over and gave her an awkward side hug. "I'm glad you're here, Kit-Kat."

She gave me a doubtful look. "Really?"

"Really," I said, pulling back but keeping my arm partially draped over her shoulders. "It's a relief to have a break from Serious, Serious-er, and Serious-est out there. At least with you here I know I'll have someone to laugh with."

She perked up visibly. "Why *are* they all always so serious, anyway?" She smiled wanly and tucked her phone into her jeans pocket. "I mean, what's the point in living forever if you're allergic to fun?"

I snorted and rolled my eyes. "I'm not positive"—I met her gaze conspiratorially—"considering I'm only eight months into forever, but I'm starting to think that the definition of 'fun' changes several centuries in. We'll catch up eventually."

"Or we'll remind them of how they used to be," Kat said, her eyes twinkling. All signs of glassy-eyed sadness were gone, her luster and spunk returned in full-force.

At a tap on the window on my side, we both jumped. Nik gave the "all clear" thumbs-up, and Kat and I pushed open our doors.

"In the future, maybe try *not* to give the pregnant invalid a heart attack," I muttered to Nik.

He blinked, his expression blank. "I never said you were an invalid." He shut the Range Rover's door as I adjusted my patchwork leather shoulder bag and looked around for Dominic. "I believe that was your word . . . that you've now used twice."

"I said I wasn't one and that's not the point," I said in a huff, crossing my arms over my chest.

Nik paused, his hand still on the side of the car, and gave me a curious look. He cocked his head to the side and took a step toward me, his irises fading from pale blue to opalescent white as Re took over. "Are you feeling alright, Alexandra? You seem unusually agitated today. Is it the hormones?"

"Duuuuude," Kat said as she rounded the back of the Range Rover. "You did *not* just tell a pregnant lady she's being too hormonal, did you?"

I looked from Kat to Re-Nik to Kat and back, then blew out a breath. "He did, but it's okay—he's right." I relaxed my arms at my sides and shook my head. "I don't know if it's the hormones, or what, but . . ." I shrugged. "The past few nights I've had this dream . . . about an accident that happened right there," I said, pointing to the spot by the road some fifty yards away. "I had the same dream last year—it was my first echo, and it was of a possible future that never actually happened, but still . . . the dream was troubling and I've been on edge ever since, like I'm waiting for the accident to really happen, which is ridiculous, because it was supposed to happen last winter, and *it never did.*" I hiked my bag up higher on my shoulder. "And I guess being here is just making me antsier. So, yeah . . ."

"You dreamed of this bygone possibility last night, you said?" Re-Nik asked.

Biting my lip, I nodded.

"Was it simply a regular dream, or an At-dream?"

"Well . . ." I frowned. "Honestly, it felt like an At-dream."

Re-Nik's eyes narrowed, the corners of his mouth turning down in a frown. "Such a thing should be impossible, and I do not use that word lightly."

"What do you mean?" I asked, not sure I wanted the answer.

Re-Nik took his time, filling the silence with more thoughtful squinting and a several-thousand-mile stare. "All unfulfilled future possibilities disappear from the At the moment they are passed by." He paused for several heartbeats, and it felt like forever. "I know this may sound confusing, but that echo—a bygone possibility of a future that never happened—should not exist anymore."

"So it was just a dream then," Kat said. "Case closed."

Both of them stared at me, waiting for a response I couldn't give them. Because I felt fairly certain that it *had* been an At-dream, and that was precisely why it had been bothering me so much. According to Re, I shouldn't have been able to view an echo of Dr. Ramirez being hit by a car last December because Dr. Ramirez *hadn't* been hit by a car, and the echo should have winked out of existence when the moment passed. And yet . . . "I, um—I'm not sure."

"You are not sure of what, Lex?" Dominic asked as he jogged around the front of the car.

"It's a long story," I said, frustration evident in my tone. I could only think of one way to set my overactive imagination and buzzing nerves to rest—I needed to venture into the At and examine the echo in question. When it showed me making my solo, uneventful trip to get coffee *without* Dr. Ramirez getting hit by a car, then I'd know once and for all that it had truly been a dream and that I was getting myself worked up over nothing.

"I have to check the At," I told the others. Upon taking in my companions' question- and doubt-filled faces, I added, "I can't explain why, but I *have* to do this."

It was Nik who nodded first, then Kat. Dominic returned my stare, his dark eyes hard, his expression set. "The At is unstable; I will accompany you."

I wasn't surprised and didn't argue. I was anxious enough about this particular trip into the At not to want to argue, and it would go a long way to setting my jumpy nerves at ease to have him there with me.

"Alright," I said, easing myself down onto the hot pavement and sitting cross-legged. I reached up for Dominic to join me on the ground, flashing him what I hoped was a reassuring smile. "Let's get this over with."

Because I felt certain that as soon as I proved to myself that all was as it should be, the mounting sense of waiting for something to happen would evaporate. All of this echo-dream dread and confusion would be behind us, and we'd be able to enjoy ourselves, worry free. I felt certain of it . . . ish.

4

SEE & BELIEVE

"Oh my God, Dr. Ramirez!" Horrified and filled with disbelief so intense it was verging on denial, I watched a past version of myself stumble toward my graduate advisor's lifeless body. This couldn't be happening. There was no way. Except it was *happening. Right before my eyes, some false version of the past was playing out in an echo that* couldn't *exist. Unless . . .*

I froze the impossible echo and turned to face Dominic. Our hands were linked, enabling us to maintain our connection in the echo—a necessity now that the At was far from stable. "It could be a false echo," I told him. "Someone could've created the whole thing."

Dominic pressed his lips together, thinning them further, and scanned the paused scene surrounding us. "Possibly, but it does not have the feel of a false echo," he said. And he would know. We both had the somewhat rare ability to manipulate the At—create cloaks to hide something in an echo or fabricate whole, new echoes entirely—but Dominic had a lot more experience with the skill, more than four centuries' worth of experience.

"Well . . ." I pursed my lips and moved them from side to side as I thought. A drizzle of rain trailed within arm's distance in front of me, and I reached out to tap the delicate strand of frozen-in-time water, what looked like the most delicate icicle in existence. "If someone created a false

echo in this time and place, for whatever reason, it's much more likely that they altered the echo because of my presence, not because of Dr. Ramirez's, don't you think?"

Dominic nodded slowly. "Considering you're not only Nejerette but the Meswett, yes, I'd say that's a fair assumption."

"Good, that's good," I said, some of the threads of worry that had wrapped around my heart loosening. This was about me, not Dr. Ramirez. For whatever reason, that made me feel better. And yet, those strands of worry were still there, intermixed with doubt and dread. I offered Dominic a wan smile. "Still, wouldn't hurt to check how far this thing reaches"

Dominic frowned, just a little, but before he could say anything, I jumped forward an hour. The echo darkened as the day grew later. It was no longer raining, but the street and sidewalks were still wet, the red, blue, and white police and ambulance lights reflecting on their shimmering surfaces.

Because according to this echo, the accident had still happened. My heart clenched.

Abandoning this location, I switched my focus to Dr. Ramirez himself. Like my grandfather, Alexander, I was a tracker—if I focused on any specific person or object, I could track said person or object through the entire span of time the person or object had existed. Finding when Dr. Ramirez popped back into existence seemed to me the simplest way to figure out how far-reaching this mangled portion of the At truly was.

Except Dr. Ramirez supposedly didn't exist during the rest of the day of the accident, or the day after. Taking a deep breath, I closed my eyes and squeezed Dominic's hand. On our own, we were each extremely powerful Nejerets, thanks to Set's almost pristine bloodline, but when our bas worked together, when we pooled our Nejeret power, our collective control over the At was pretty damn flawless. And with the At's current instability, that was something I needed right about now.

I pushed forward in time, keeping my focus on Dr. Ramirez. He continued to not *exist the days following the accident, and the week after. He didn't exist a month out, or two months . . . or three.*

"This can't be happening," I said, panic making my voice thready. "Nobody would go to the trouble to erase him like this—it would take forever *to do this."*

"It's been done before," Dominic said, his thickening accent telling me that he was battling his own growing concern.

*"Yeah, but that was Hitler. Apep wanted the chaos he would bring to the world . . . but Dr. Ramirez is just a professor of archaeology. What could he possibly do in the future that would make someone—*anyone*—want to hide his actions by erasing his existence from the day of the 'accident' on?"*

"It is impossible to see that which has been hidden," Dominic said. "I do not mean to trouble you further, Lex, but is it possible that something has since happened to your Dr. Ramirez, and that only a small period of time was altered in the At?"

I shook my head adamantly. "He's not really dead, Dom. I mean, we just exchanged emails a few days ago." I fought my rising panic. "He's the whole reason this day trip turned into a group excursion rather than just Neffe coming out here to do her research alone." I was fully aware that Dominic knew all of this, but some part of me was convinced that if my words could banish the doubt in his midnight eyes, everything would be alright.

Dominic hesitated to speak, but his lips eventually parted, and the words that left his mouth elicited a whole new maelstrom of panic. "Anyone can send an email, Lex . . . they just need access to the account."

5

BAD & WORSE

"Lex, wait!" Dominic yelled after me as I raced across the small parking lot toward the pathway that edged around the side of Denny Hall.

"I have to know," I shouted over my shoulder, my sandals slapping against the asphalt.

"Know what?" Nik asked a moment before his hand latched onto my arm and he pulled me to a halt. I was still a few strides from the curb, couldn't even see the steep steps leading up to the anthropology building's front doors, and acting on instinct I yanked to free my arm. The attempt was pointless; Nik's grip was unyielding.

"I have to make sure he's okay," I told my ancient friend, pleading with my voice and eyes and more useless tugs against his grip. "Let go, Nik, please."

"Do *not* let her go," Dominic said as he strode toward us, Kat close behind him. "She could be running into a trap. I can't believe we were so careless."

Nik's expression hardened. "What did you find in the At?"

"Let me go and I'll tell you," I said, feeling both obstinate and defeated. Dominic was right—my instinctive reaction had been reckless and would've endangered not only myself but Marcus and our unborn children, as well. I pressed my free hand against my lower abdomen in silent apology.

Not a heartbeat later, I caught the eye of a lone coed crossing the mouth of the small lot. She pulled her phone out of her back pocket, her face an open question. Did I need help? Should she call the police? Considering Nik's appearance and the way he was restraining me, not to mention Dominic and Kat's presence nearby, almost looking like they'd come over to suss out the situation, I couldn't blame the young woman for jumping to such conclusions.

I shook my head at her, offering her a small smile of thanks. Between clenched teeth, I said, "Let go, Nik, before someone tries to play hero . . ."

Nik's eyes tensed, but he did let go. After he'd stepped around me to block my access to the pathway, of course. Despite my title of Meswett, prophesied girl-child and savior to our people, and my honorary position on the Council of Seven, sometimes I felt more like a prisoner than a leader. And by sometimes, I meant most of the time. How well the Council had ignored my input this morning about their debate over Re-Nik joining them being an exercise in futility was further proof of that.

Nik leaned in closer to me, his words as sharp and heated as the determination in his pale blue eyes. "Everything I do, I do to keep you safe. Everything." His unwavering gaze shifted from me to Dominic and back. "Now tell me what happened in the At."

I quickly relayed what we had—and hadn't—discovered, making sure he understood just how important it was to me to make sure Dr. Ramirez was okay. One way or another, I was determined to get eyes into Denny Hall to check on him.

Nik was quiet for a long moment, then let out a heavy sigh.

"Sorry, Lex, but I'm inclined to agree with Dom here, and so is Re. There's no way you're going in there now."

"But—"

Nik crossed his arms, flashing me one of his fresher tattoos—an evergreen tree line ringing his forearm in an array of black and grays.

Shoulders slumping, I slunk away from him toward our car and settled, once more, on the sun-warmed asphalt. Part of me was starting to wonder if they were right, if something had happened to Dr. Ramirez, something hidden under the apparent cluster of false echoes, and the person I'd been emailing with to set up this meeting had, in reality, been an imposter.

Dominic followed me and stood between me and the midday sun, his shadow a cool contrast to the warm asphalt. "Do you still have his number, Lex?"

I looked up at him, eyebrows raised in question. "Dr. Ramirez's?"

He nodded.

"Yes."

"Well, it's simple then." Dominic sat on the ground beside me. It was the perfect balm for my agitated mood—his presence always had an almost magically calming effect on my troubled soul. "Call Dr. Ramirez," he said. "If he answers, then we'll know he's alright and that the meeting is benign enough."

I searched his eyes, the blackish-brown hue of his irises speckled with bronze in the sunlight, seeking answers he couldn't know. "But the At . . . even if he answers, something's still wrong with what the At *thinks* happened last winter."

Dominic's shoulders rose and fell and his head moved from side to side. "It's something we'll have analyzed when we get back."

"But—but—"

"It'll be okay, Lex," Kat said, sitting on the ground on the other side of me and taking my hand in hers. "We'll figure this out."

Nik took several steps toward the nearest pine tree in the foliage bordering the lot and placed his hand against its rough bark. "I have, in rare occasions in the past, noticed an odd occurrence when certain of my more notable and powerful descendants manifested." From the accent and cadence of his words, it was obvious that Re had taken over. "They create something of a disturbance in the At surrounding the first few echoes they viewed. It happened with Nik, of course," Re-Nik said, touching his own chest, "as well as with all of my direct children and some of their children, such as Heru, Aset, and Set. Over time, I came to believe that it meant those individuals would have a distinct effect on the events to come, that their presence in the At would be disproportionately significant."

My eyebrows drew together. "So you think because that echo with Dr. Ramirez getting hit by a car was the first one I viewed, I might have disrupted it to the point of changing all of the following related echoes as well?" It sounded like a stretch to me, but then, so did my whole life.

"I have never seen such a far-reaching disruption, but considering your significance to maintaining ma'at—universal balance quite literally depends on the fates of you and the children you carry—I can't bring myself to believe that such a large disturbance in the At is out of the realm of possibility." The answer was so much like Nuin—Re's original Nejeret host—that my heart warmed. Nuin had always had the damndest time admitting that he simply didn't know something.

I smiled to myself and reached into my bag to fish out my phone. "Okay, so I call Dr. Ramirez, and let's say he answers . . . then what?" After unlocking my phone, I scrolled through the contacts until I reached the Ds. "Are we still suspicious of foul play at that point, or can we assume this is simply a harmless meeting and we can all go into Denny?" I gave Kat's hand a squeeze. "Does Kit-Kat still get the grand tour?"

I watched Dominic and Nik exchange a prolonged glance, watched Nik's irises bleed back to their usual pale blue hue. Finally, Nik shook his head. "It's not worth the risk, Lex. Ask him to meet you somewhere else . . . somewhere crowded with humans."

Nodding slowly, I thought about where to propose Dr. Ramirez meet with me, my thumb hovering over the green call button. I considered the HUB and By George, the two main places to eat on campus—it was after noon, and we'd planned to eat before the meeting anyway. A hungry Nejeret is a grumpy Nejeret, after all.

The Husky Union Building, affectionately called the HUB by anybody who knew anything at all about the U, would likely be more crowded, since it was lunchtime and there were more dining options in comparison to By George—aptly named due to its proximity to a rather prominent statue of George Washington—and its cafeteria-style dining. But the HUB was also clear across campus, which I doubted would please my not unwanted but very overprotective bodyguards. There was also the nearby Burke Café, but it was tiny and rarely crowded.

Suddenly, an idea struck me and I sat up straighter, smiling broadly. It was so obvious; I couldn't believe I hadn't thought of it right away. "I know just the place."

It had been ages since I'd been in Suzzallo Library—okay, maybe only months, but it felt like ages when I was used to spending hours there every day, hunting through the stacks or hunched over a wooden desk with a wall of rarely opened books blocking me off from the world. The café on the first floor would serve our dining purposes well enough—it had a full-service coffee bar and grab-and-go sandwiches, pastries, and snacks—but it would also give me a chance to show Kat around one of my favorite places on campus. One day all of this universe-atstake hoopla would be over, and she'd go to college like a normal kid, and I'd be damned if I didn't try my hardest to convince her to become a Husky.

I pressed my thumb to the screen and called Dr. Ramirez.

After three rings with no answer, I held my breath. After the fourth, I squeezed my eyes shut, and after the fifth, my heart was beating so hard it felt like it was pounding against my ribcage.

"You've reached the mailbox for 206-555-0173," said the emotionless automatic recording. "The caller you're trying to reach is not available. Please leave a message at the tone."

Panicking, I ended the call before the beep. I looked at Dominic, then up at Nik, knowing they'd heard the impersonal recording as well. "At least the number's not disconnected," I said softly. It was the only thing I could think to point out that didn't lend further credence to the possibility that something had happened to Dr. Ramirez and that this whole "meeting" was just an elaborate ruse. A trap.

"I think you should get back into the car, Lex," Nik said, turning his back to me so he could scan the countless trees and shrubs scattered nearby for potential dangers.

I didn't even consider arguing. There was no point, and he was right—the situation was looking grimmer and grimmer with each passing minute. I was on my feet, my hand on the door handle, when my phone buzzed twice to alert me of a text message.

Hastily, I unlocked the phone and opened the message. It was from Dr. Ramirez. Or, at least, it was from his number.

Sorry I missed your call, Lex. Is everything alright? Do you need to reschedule? I had a cancellation, so my whole afternoon is free, if another time works better for you.

. . .

I STARED AT THE PHONE'S SCREEN, DIM IN THE bright sunlight, my hands shaking. I could feel Kat behind me, reading over my shoulder.

"Um . . . why didn't he just call you back?" Kat's voice wavered a little. "Am I the only one wondering that?"

"No," I said under my breath. "No, you're not."

6

AH... & AWE

"Hello? Lex?"

I exhaled heavily upon hearing Dr. Ramirez's deep, familiar voice. "Hey, Dr. Ramirez!" I took a deep breath to calm my frazzled nerves. "Sorry to keep calling you, but texts haven't been getting through on my phone lately," I lied. "And, well . . . it's a long story."

"It's alright, Lex." I thought I could hear a smile in his voice. "I'm on a conference call right now, so . . ." Such a simple explanation as to why he hadn't answered the first time.

"Oh my gosh, I'm sorry! I'll make it quick, then." I relayed my request for the change in meeting locale and let him know that I had a bit of an entourage with me, and when Dr. Ramirez agreed to the new plans, we said our goodbyes so he could return to his call.

Practically giddy with relief, I turned around to grin at my companions. "So *that's* good news." I looked from Nik to Dominic and back, knowing they'd heard everything Dr. Ramirez had said on the phone. "Right?"

They might not have been overly enthusiastic about it, but they did both nod. Eventually.

"Okay, so . . . we're good, right? We can head down to the library and get settled in for the meeting?" My stomach grumbled. "And eat."

Again, Nik and Dominic gave their reluctant nods. They moved so similarly it almost appeared rehearsed.

"Good," I said with a heavy exhale. After tucking my phone back into my bag, I linked my arm with Kat's and started toward the sidewalk that led to the stairway down to Red Square and across the expansive brick plaza, to Suzzallo Library. My spirits were the highest they'd been all day, and I didn't want to waste a minute more of our oh-so-rare free day now that we'd banished *most* of the dark clouds.

"So where we're going now is one of my very favorite places on campus," I told Kat, squeezing her arm to hug her a little closer as we wound around a roundabout and headed toward the school's main flagpole. "It's just so . . . I don't know." I tossed her a sideways glance, meeting her bemused eyes. "I remember the first time I came here—it was for a middle school field trip, and my mom was my group's chaperone."

As we reached the broad cement stairs leading down to Red Square, I leaned in closer, like I was going to share a secret. "She was a Husky, too," I said, then straightened. "So she had all kinds of stories that made this place seem magical. It was like getting a chance to glimpse into her past." I snorted. "Ironically enough . . ." I shook my head. "But anyway, Suzzallo was the place she was most excited to show me, because she knew how much I'd love it because it basically looks like an old castle."

We reached the bottom of the stairs and stepped onto red bricks whose color had been dulled by the span of dry heat we'd been having. Passing between aluminum bike racks and a row of alternating purple and gold flags boasting the benefits of attending the U to new and prospective students, we made our way into Red Square. A few moments later, I pointed ahead to where part of the grand old library was coming into view behind

Kane Hall, made only more majestic in comparison to Kane's blocky cement colonnade and overall general hideousness.

"And there it is," I said quietly, "dear old Suzzallo."

"You know," Kat said, "I *have* been here before. Like every year we'd take a field trip here and learn about all the history and stuff."

I looked at her, shaken out of my nostalgic reverie, and grinned. "Of course you have, but you've never been here *with me*, and that's an entirely different thing."

She looked at me, a single eyebrow raised. Lucky girl to get that gene when it had passed me by without a second glance. "Why's that?"

"Because I'm not going to tell you the history." A little bounce entered my step as we drew nearer to the library's arched doorways, the central figures in Suzzallo's elaborate Gothic façade. "I'm going to help you *feel* the history of this place. And it's so much more than that—it's the beauty of knowing how much knowledge has passed through its doors, transported in the minds of students and researchers, the appreciation and awe that comes with understanding just how purposeful each and every piece of architecture and decoration is and how each element represents not only academia and discovery, but this crazy unique place we call home.

"I mean—" I stopped in the middle of the nearly empty brick plaza and gestured to the stairs that led away from Red Square to the south end of campus. Tree-lined brick buildings bordered a wide walkway leading to a large, circular fountain surrounded by a sea of rose bushes. Beyond that, the horizon was decorated with two staples of the Puget Sound area: never-ending evergreen-covered foothills and majestic Mt. Rainier, grand as ever against a backdrop of clear blue summer sky. "There's nowhere else in the world like this."

There was a reason Marcus had chosen to establish his line's main complex in the Puget Sound despite his propensity to grumble about the prominent damp chill that lasted full-on half of the year—it was so damn beautiful. And I could see in Kat's rich brown eyes that she understood, maybe better than either Marcus or I ever could, because she was from here. This place was in her bones, in her blood. It was her home.

"Well, come on," she said, tugging on my arm and dragging me onward toward the library. "Now that you've got me all excited to *feel the history*, let's get this show on the road already!"

I laughed and, more than willing, let her tug me toward Suzzallo. Glancing over my shoulder, I spotted Nik hanging back several dozen yards, seeming to watch everything and nothing at the same time, but I didn't see Dominic anywhere.

At spotting my quizzical expression, Nik nodded toward the library, and I understood. The other half of my minimal guard for the day had gone inside to scope out any potential dangers before I stepped through the front doors. Duh.

Once we were inside in the foyer, the muffled echo of voices surrounded us. A buzzing tour group huddled together further in the library where the 1970s addition joined up with the original 1920s structure, and people sitting in clusters in the cavernous café to the right of the foyer shared hushed conversation over iced coffees and laptops.

Kat had been in the library before, but never as a Nejerette, and I couldn't help but wonder if that added to her rapt expression as she took it all in. She was especially intrigued by the shallow grooves worn into the travertine steps of the split grand staircase from thousands upon thousands of library-goers ascending and descending the twin curving, carved stone stairways over the past century, though she also "oohed" a bit at the elaborate leaded glass windows stretching high overhead in the walls sheltering the staircases.

"I think I get what you mean about the 'feel' of it," she whispered. "It's like I'm at Hogwarts or something," she added with a giggle, placing her hand over her mouth when the sound echoed more than she'd expected.

Dominic stood at the top of the stairway, his back to us as he waited for us to finish our ascent. I touched his arm as I passed him, offering a quick smile before moving on. He nodded, his deep-set eyes filled with secrets but his face stony. "Ah, Lex?" he said quietly.

I paused and turned around partially to face him, motioning for Kat to continue on.

"The Reading Room is safe enough, but please don't venture into the stacks at all." He tilted his head minutely toward the newer portion of the library, an aisle running between bookcase after bookcase in a seemingly endless optical illusion. "Too many hiding places for my comfort." Though his words had sounded like a polite request, I knew them to be much more. Don't go into the stacks. Noted.

"No problem," I told him, flashing him another smile, tighter this time. "Thanks."

I found Kat standing in one of two doorways to the Reading Room, which was, in my opinion, one of the most beautiful and relaxing places to research in the entire world. It was one of the few places I'd ever been where the rule of quiet was obeyed universally, as though even raucous coeds could sense the volume of knowledge and wisdom that had been absorbed under its vaulted ceiling.

I stopped beside Kat in the doorway and leaned my shoulder against the wooden doorframe. "So what do you think?" I asked her in the barest whisper. "Worthy of a sketch or two?"

She nodded, eyes wide as she took it all in. "It reminds me of those cathedrals in Florence," she whispered, "except warmer, like here they actually want me to sit down and stay for a while."

I smiled broadly, having felt exactly the same way about this room from the moment I first set eyes on it as a young teen. When my phone buzzed, I fished it out of my bag and glanced at the screen; it was Dr. Ramirez.

Before answering, I pointed to the carved wooden bookshelves bordering the room and whispered, "Check out the friezes on top of the bookcases." At Kat's confused look, I amended, "The carvings—they're all of flora native to this area. It's pretty cool." I watched Kat's face brighten with understanding as I backed out into the landing and answered my phone.

"Hey, Dr. Ramirez," I said, still keeping my voice hushed. I hurried past Dominic and the staircase and into an off-shooting hallway that led to the restrooms, where I could speak above a whisper without bothering anyone.

"Ah, Lex, so glad you answered," he said. "I don't, by any chance, suppose you're already on campus?"

"Actually, I am."

"Well then, I'm heading to Suzzallo right now. Think you'd be able to move our meeting up a half hour?" A muffled laugh made its way across the line. "This is the last thing on my calendar today, and with the rest of the day unexpectedly free, I thought I'd take advantage of the sunshine and head home afterwards to get a full afternoon of gardening in."

The mental image of big, burly Dr. Ramirez rolling up his shirtsleeves and getting dirty in a flowerbed was enough to make me grin. "Yeah, of course. I'm actually already here. I'll meet you in the café in a few minutes."

I emerged from the hallway to find Kat and Dominic waiting for me at the top of the nearest staircase. And for some strange reason, that eerie sense of waiting had a resurgence. Or maybe it had been there all along, but wanting to enjoy at least part of the day, I'd been too stubborn to acknowledge it. *It's just the weirdness in the At,* I told myself. And the dream and my hormones and, as much as I hated to admit it, being away from Marcus. It was a perfect recipe for a crappy day.

I took a deep breath, then forced a smile. "Who's hungry?"

7

TICK & BOOM

"Egypt certainly seems to have agreed with you," Dr. Ramirez said after releasing me from a body-engulfing grandfatherly hug. His soft brown eyes scanned my face. "You look absolutely radiant."

"Oh, well . . ." I glanced down at the floor and felt my face heat. Gracefully accepting compliments had never been my strong suit, a facet of my personality that appeared to intrigue Marcus.

"That's because she's pr—" Kat slapped her hands over her mouth. When I glanced down at her with what could only be called "a look," I found laughter and apologies dancing in her eyes.

"Dr. Ramirez," I said through a slightly forced smile. I placed my hand on Kat's shoulder—she was seated with Dominic at the good-sized square table we'd claimed a couple minutes earlier, my chair beside hers and the extra for Dr. Ramirez opposite her currently empty. "This is my youngest sister, Kat."

"It's nice to meet you, Kat," Dr. Ramirez said, offering her his hand. She looked a little stumped, but just for a moment, before reaching out to shake hands. "For whatever reason," he said when they'd finished, "I was under the impression that you only had the one sister." He frowned thoughtfully. "Hmm . . . Jenny, if I'm correct?"

"I did only have the one sister," I said, motioning to his free chair before pulling out my own to sit. "Or, at least, I thought I did." I glanced at Kat, meeting her eyes and smiling fondly. "Kat's my half-sister, and we just found out about each other a few months back." I let out a breathy laugh. "It's a long story," I said, shaking my head. And complicated. And absolutely, completely unbelievable.

"It would seem that you're full of long stories today." Before he sat, Dr. Ramirez pulled a slender, polished wooden box out of his leather briefcase and set it on the table.

The feeling of waiting—what I was now starting to recognize as a strange mixture of dread and expectation—quadrupled with that single action. It was like a timer was ticking, counting down to something, only I didn't know how long it would tick for or what would happen when it stopped. It just kept on ticking and ticking and ticking, silent and unsettling.

Dr. Ramirez rested his bag on the floor and eased himself down into his chair. My eyes were glued to the slim wooden box, but he didn't notice, as he was too focused on something else. I forced my gaze to break away from the box to see what had captured his attention.

It was Nik. Of course.

Walking around with Nik was the opposite of camouflage, but in some ways, that was better than trying to hide. He was one of those people who was always gawked at, but those same gawkers usually went out of their way to ignore him. The same thing that made him stand out often rendered him all but invisible. He was the guy with the piercings and tattoos. That was all most people saw. It was all most people *wanted* to see. A sad notion, but sadder still was my suspicion that it was all Nik wanted people to see when they looked at him. His appearance was a barrier between himself and the world—by choice. I didn't get it, and unlike most of the Nejerets who weren't too afraid of him to talk about him, I didn't pretend to.

At the moment, my confounding friend was returning from the coffee bar with a monstrous energy drink, a plastic-wrapped sandwich, and a couple of large cookies, everyone around him either watching him or trying to appear disinterested. He sat two tables away, seeming to ignore us completely as he kept an eye on everyone else in the room.

I met Dr. Ramirez's speculative eyes and shrugged. He smiled faintly and shook his head, his eyebrows quirked together as if to say, "Kids these days . . ."

"Trust me," I told him, "I don't get it either." As I spoke, my stomach rumbled quietly—apparently triggered by the sight of Nik's food—and almost instantly, Dominic pushed his chair back and stood.

"What can I get everyone to eat?" he asked, his accent elevating his polite demeanor to the next level.

Remembering my rusty manners, I cleared my throat. "Dr. Ramirez, you remember Dominic l'Aragne from the Djeser-Djeseru excavation crew, don't you? I'm sure your paths must've crossed at some point while we were holed up in Denny . . ."

"Why yes, yes, I do remember seeing you around." Dr. Ramirez stood and shook the younger-appearing man's hand. "I knew you looked familiar, but I couldn't place you. It's great to see you again."

"And you as well, professor." A smile softened his severe features, and he bowed his head minutely. "Now what can I get you for lunch?"

Dr. Ramirez paused halfway in the act of sitting back down. "Oh, no, you don't need to do—"

"Please," I said, placing my fingertips on his forearm. "It's our treat . . . for everything you've done for me over the past few years."

He met my smile with an awkward one of his own and lowered himself down the rest of the way into his chair. "Well, alright, but only this once." He gave Dominic his order, which I followed up with "the usual"—a turkey sandwich, a scone, and large decaf vanilla latte—and Kat requested, "PB & J—anything red—and a chocolate chip cookie. And some hot Cheetos. And a Coke—a Cherry Coke."

While Dominic was fetching lunch, Dr. Ramirez and I did the catching-up dance—how have you been and what's new and the like—but finally I had to interrupt our conversation to look at Kat, who was literally bouncing in her seat. "What is up with you?"

"How have you not told him yet?" she all but exploded.

My eyes opened wide. "Told him *what*?" I asked, astonished. She couldn't possibly have expected me to divulge the past eight months' happenings—Nejeret matters, time travel, and all—to my former, very human graduate advisor.

"About"—she glanced down at my middle—"you know . . ."

"Oh! Right," I said, smacking my forehead at my denseness. "I'm pregnant." The words came out blasé, but the moment they were free, I blushed. Because to get pregnant, as everyone knows, you had to have sex. Which meant I'd basically just told Dr. Ramirez that I'd had sex. Which was just awkward.

"Well, uh, congratulations . . ." He looked from me to Kat and back, clearly uncomfortable. Apparently he found it awkward, too. "I'm assuming?"

"Oh, yeah," Kat said. "It's not one of those *whoopsie* things. I mean, it kind of is, but they're stoked about it, anyway."

Dr. Ramirez's responding grin was full and warm. "Congratulations. You two make a handsome couple," he said, glancing to the line at the coffee bar, where Dominic was standing with a food-filled wire basket in his arms, next to pay.

"Dom?" I said, surprised, and Kat snorted unabashedly. "Oh, no, we're not—he's not—he's just my—" Half-brother I didn't know about last year? Best friend? Bodyguard? Platonic soul mate? "Friend," I said lamely, because he was so much more.

"Oh, I'm sorry," Dr. Ramirez said. "I just assumed . . ." He shifted in his seat, shaking his head. "This is a bit embarrassing."

"It's fine," I told him. "Dom and I are really close friends, but I'm actually engaged to Marcus Bahur . . . the Djeser-Djeseru excavation director." I chuckled to myself. "So, uh, thanks for recommending me for the position on the excavation . . ."

Dr. Ramirez laughed out loud and, much to my amusement, actually slapped his knee. "Well, how about that! Never knew I had a future in matchmaking." His smile was broad, warm, and catching. Kat and I were grinning along with him almost immediately.

But as my eyes were once again drawn to the small wooden box, my smile wilted.

Tick . . . tick . . . tick . . .

"Ah, yes!" Dr. Ramirez pushed the box across the corner of the table to me. "This. I forgot about it in the excitement of everything."

I made small, interested noises, once again forcing myself to look away from the box despite my desire to do nothing but stare at it, especially now that it was close enough to me that I could almost make out a shadow of my reflection on its surface. Part of me expected it to open a yawning mouth and lunge at me in an attempt to bite my face off. Another part of me wanted to open it more than I'd ever wanted to open anything, because I was fairly certain opening the damn box would be the only way to make the sense of waiting—the silent ticking—finally stop.

"So what's in it, anyway?" Kat asked. Her words seemed to jog me out of a trance.

I placed my fingertips on the edge of the box and slid it closer to me. "And what's the story behind it?" I looked at Dr. Ramirez. "All you said in your email was that you had an artifact for me, something with me 'written all over it.'"

Dr. Ramirez nodded slowly. "Right, well . . ." He reached out and tapped the polished lid. "This little gem here actually came to me with a note inside, just two words written on it."

Both Kat and I leaned forward, waiting.

Tick . . . tick . . . tick . . .

Dr. Ramirez's warm brown eyes met mine, his eyebrows raised. "Alexandra Larson."

Slowly, my stare dropped to the box, and I fought the urge to shiver. The expectant sensation was nearly overwhelming now, the silent ticking almost deafening.

"Ohmigod, open it, Lex," Kat said, squirming in her seat. She was gripping the edge of the table, her fingertips pressing against the surface so hard they were bleaching of color. "All this mystery . . . I seriously can't handle it!"

Neither could I.

Tick . . . tick . . . tick . . .

The lid creaked faintly as I opened it. The sense of waiting, of expectation, turned to full-on dread and, as I rested the lid on the tabletop, to near-outright revulsion. It was a struggle to keep my expression curious, interested, to fight the urge to slam the lid closed and throw the repulsive thing across the room while brushing off the sudden tidal wave of heebie-jeebies like so much raw sewage.

Because I had absolutely no reason to feel that way about what was in the box. I would have no way to explain my totally bizarre reaction to *it*.

And, possibly most disturbing of all, the ticking in my head hadn't stopped when I'd opened the box. It had only grown louder, become truly audible.

"What is it?" Kat asked, her voice filled with nothing but curiosity and maybe a hint of disappointment. "A compass?"

I shook my head, leaning in to get a closer look despite my urge to fling the box away. "It's a watch . . . a pocket watch." Couldn't she hear it ticking? It sounded so loud to me, overwhelming all the other sounds in the room as I stared at the device nestled snugly in a padded gray velvet depression.

The watch was made of some dark metal that had been treated in a way that caused it to appear nearly black. I squinted, my mouth quirked to the side. Not nearly black—the thing was pitch-black, its dull metal surface not reflecting light but seeming to consume it. The sense of revulsion it instilled within me wasn't based on how it looked—rather, the watch was a breathtakingly beautiful creation, its black filigree design undeniably delicate and feminine—but from something deeper. It was instinctive, a gut feeling.

This pocket watch was wrong, or *off*. Its very existence clashed with my internal sense of balance. *Of ma'at,* I realized, pressing my palm against my abdomen as though I could somehow draw strength of will and clarity of mind from the two souls within, the living embodiment of universal balance.

"What's it look like on the inside?" Kat asked, reaching out to touch the watch's black filigree cover.

Breath catching, I snapped the lid of the box shut and raised my head, meeting her eyes. I didn't know what would've happened if she'd touched the watch, but I had the visceral sense that touching it would be a very, very bad thing.

"Lex?" Her brows drew together, her eyes filled with worry. "Are you okay? You're so pale . . ."

"I—" I cleared my throat and licked my lips. "I'm feeling a little light-headed," I said truthfully. "I think I just need to eat something."

"Yes, yes, of course," Dr. Ramirez said gruffly. "Let's let the mother-to-be eat before we get too sidetracked by our mysterious artifact here."

I looked at my old advisor, giving him a weak, grateful smile. His expression was wrought with concern, but his eyes weren't troubled like Kat's. I glanced two tables over.

Or Nik's.

8

MATTER & ANTIMATTER

"It really was good to see you," I told Dr. Ramirez while I hugged him goodbye, meaning the words with all my heart. Not only had it been nice to catch up, but I felt a huge relief having actually seen my former advisor in the flesh. Whatever was happening to him in the At, Dr. Ramirez was okay in the real, tangible world, and that was what truly mattered.

He returned my sentiment and said his farewells and nice-to-meet-yous, and I remained standing as I watched him weave his way between occupied and vacant tables and walk out through the café's wide entrance. Only when he was finally out of sight, having passed through the library's glass doors, did I sit back down, stiff as a mummy. My relief at his well-being was eclipsed by the wrongness emanating from the graceful little box sitting in the middle of the table, surrounded by a moat of food wrappers, napkins, drink bottles, and coffee cups.

"Are you going to fill me in on what's bothering you, or must I guess?" Dominic asked from the opposite side of the table.

I met his dark, worried eyes. "It's that thing," I said, pointing to the box. "It feels . . ." I shuddered. "Wrong. It just feels wrong, somehow . . . like a really disturbing sucking void of, I don't know, *wrongness*." I met Kat's eyes. "Didn't you feel it?"

She quirked her mouth to the side and shook her head. "But it's just a pocket watch." Pushing her lunch trash to the corner of the table, she reached for the box.

I grabbed hold of her wrist without thought, and she looked at me with widened eyes. "I don't think you should touch it," I told her, trying to smooth out the alarm tensing my features. "I don't think *anyone* should touch it."

Nik slid into Dr. Ramirez's abandoned chair and leaned his forearms on the table, getting a closer look at the harmless-looking box. "And why's that?" He cocked his head to the side and pulled back a bit. "You sensed something when you opened it—that much was obvious. Is it made of At?"

"No," Kat said, voicing my slight head shake. "It's black. It's kinda pretty, though . . . in a weird way."

Frowning, I stared at the box. The watch was pretty, what with all that delicate filigree work and the striking black metal. But any attraction it held was far overshadowed by its repulsive wrongness.

"What is it?" Dominic said, and I glanced up at him, only to follow his wary line of sight to Nik's face. He was absolutely still, his expression blank and his gaze distant.

In a blink, his irises flashed from pale blue to opalescent white, and his gaze locked on me. I saw an emotion I'd never seen in those eyes, set in either Nik's or Nuin's face: horror.

Slowly, Re-Nik reached out and lifted the lid of the box. The ticking intensified once more, as did the wrongness pouring out of the watch in wave after repellant wave. He stared at the small, black soul-sore for several seconds, then sighed and gently lowered the lid. "Perhaps I should have anticipated this, but . . ." He shook his head, his eyes downcast. "I was unaware that any Nejeret alive had developed the ability to create such a thing." He looked at me again, his gaze beseeching. "It *shouldn't* be possible."

"Re," I said, drawing out the entity-in-charge's name. "You're doing that thing where you only say really vague and cryptic things again . . ."

"Oh my God, totally," Kat exclaimed. "I'm glad it's not just me."

"It's not," Dominic said, with a miniscule nod of agreement. "Please, Great Father, explain to us what it is you aren't saying."

Re-Nik studied each of us in turn as he considered how to word his response. Finally, his opal eyes locked onto me, and Nik's youthful features grew weary under the weight of Re's thoughts. "Ma'at—universal balance—is not merely a concept, but a universal law of being woven through everything in existence across all dimensions, all planes . . . all universes. You, my Alexandra, are the embodiment of ma'at as you sit here today with the two driving forces of creation and destruction in this universe nestled safely in your womb, equal and opposite in power . . . balanced."

I instinctively laced my fingers together and pressed them against my abdomen. It was difficult to wrap my mind around the thought—no, the *fact*—that the children I was carrying were so terrifyingly important to, quite literally, everything.

"But ma'at is visible in a much more mundane way—everywhere and in everything," Re-Nik continued. "You are familiar with At, but less so with its counterpart: the in-between, the substance linking this moment to the next, interweaving threads of the At. There is no word for it in a human tongue, for none was ever needed, but it is the very glue holding time and space together."

Upon seeing what no doubt had to be a flabbergasted expression on my face, he leaned closer and said, "The fabric of the At alone could not sustain this." He raised his hands slightly and cast a quick glance around the room. "It would be chaos, constant change and perpetual motion that has no meaning or form or purpose. Its balancing force provides stability, opposing the At in every way. And as such, At is drawn to it, anchored by it, and the two forces combine in perfect concert." He breathed in and out slowly, studying each of our faces. "And with their marriage comes creation."

"Like matter and antimatter?" Kat asked quietly.

Ever so slowly, like a trio of unoiled marionettes, Dominic, Re-Nik, and I looked at Kat.

"You know . . . like how when an antimatter particle gets together with its matching matter twin and they, like, annihilate each other or whatever and release a bunch of energy and, um, stuff." She looked at each of us, her cheeks reddening. "What? I got a five on the AP Physics test, okay? I know stuff." Mumbling, she added, "Some stuff . . ."

"Katarina is very astute in her comparison," Re-Nik said with a conciliatory bow of his head. "In fact, I would say that the concepts of matter and antimatter are quite likely the closest modern science has yet to come to explaining ma'at."

I licked my lips and cleared my throat. "Okay . . . so this in-between antimatter stuff—is that what the watch is made of?"

Re-Nik nodded.

"And that's why it feels so . . ." I shivered melodramatically.

"Yes and no," he said. "Much like solidified At can be imbued with certain properties, such as the Hathor statuette that pulled you back to ancient times, its counterpart can be anchored to an aspect of creation, like a specific object or person. It's an aberration of ma'at, which is probably why it's disturbing the twins so much, Alexandra, that you're picking up on their discomfort."

"Hmm . . ." So my weird feeling all day really had been linked to the pregnancy, just not in the way I'd suspected. "So, what happens after this 'anchoring'?" I asked, sucking in a breath and holding it while I waited for Re-Nik to respond. Because I was fairly certain he was implying that the watch made of this in-between, anti-At stuff was anchored to Dr. Ramirez, and I was terrified to find out what that meant for the kindly old professor.

"Annihilation?" Kat said in a small voice.

"For an object or a being without a ba, no," Re-Nik said, glancing at Kat, but once again retraining his eyes on me. "Your Dr. Ramirez will be completely erased from the At, in time, but it will not affect him on this plane of existence. But—" He raised his eyebrows. "For a being *with* a ba—for any Nejeret—it is a different matter entirely. The link created by the individual's ba between the physical body on this plane and their reflection in the At would mean that once their existence was erased from the At, the same would happen to their body, here."

I swallowed roughly. "But why would someone do that to Dr. Ramirez? Why go through all the trouble to anchor this thing to him just to erase him from the At?"

"Ah, but that's just it," Re-Nik said, his voice soft, cautious . . . dangerous. "This watch wasn't created with the specific purpose of binding to your Dr. Ramirez—the desire to bond with elements of At is a basic principle of its nature. Once given solid form, it will affect anyone who touches it until it is depleted. The watch was simply created and, I'm assuming, given to Dr. Ramirez with the intention of him passing it on to you, my Alexandra. It was sheer luck that he handled it, anchoring it to the reflection of himself in the At, and that you have such a close tie to an echo containing him. It was your first, and as such, you felt it deep in your ba the moment it was altered—or in this case, the moment the echo reappeared in the At. My point is, without that particular string of events, we wouldn't have gone into this meeting on high alert, and the worst could have happened." He stared at me intently. "Any of us could have touched the watch. *You* could have . . ."

I blanched, then looked at Kat. Her face was so washed out I thought she might be seconds away from fainting. I reached for her hand under the table and gave her fingers a squeeze. "You didn't touch it," I said, aiming for reassuring but certain I'd fallen short. "You're okay."

Kat nodded, looking like she was about to throw up.

"So," Dominic started, and we all looked at him. "I'm assuming this—this *thing* didn't simply burst into existence on its own."

He'd voiced what I'd been too afraid to say aloud, and now *I* felt like I was about to throw up. "So who could've made it?"

Crickets.

A sickening thought struck me, and I licked my lips, but my mouth was so dry that it did no good. Reaching for my coffee cup, I took a drink of tepid latte. "There's no way that this could be like the Hathor statuette, could it? There's not some unexpected trip to the past scheduled in the near future, where I go back and create this thing with the sole purpose of destroying Nejerets—specifically *myself*—is there?" My voice rose in pitch as I spoke, and a slight tremble started in my hands. I let go of the coffee cup and pressed my palms against my thighs in an attempt to control the shaking.

Re-Nik took such a long time to respond that my stomach twisted into a nauseating tangle. "No, my Alexandra, the scenario as you've suggested it is impossible. Only if you had complete access to Apep's sheut would you be able to create something like this watch," he said, tapping the box's shiny lid once more. "And Apep's sheut is only compatible with humanoids carrying the Y chromosome."

Somewhere in the far recesses of my mind, I realized he'd just told me one of my children would be a boy by necessity of the sheut that would be bound through every particle of his being.

"So, either the future carrier of Apep's sheut is responsible for this," Re-Nik said, "or Nik, here, is not the only Nejeret to have been born with his own sheut."

"But I thought you kept that from happening," I said, panic and disbelief battling for control in my chest. "You policed the timeline yourself to make sure no other kids were born of two Nejeret parents."

Re-Nik stared at me for several seconds, and then he shrugged. He *shrugged*. His only response to the possibility that he might've failed in one of his self-proclaimed most important tasks and allowed the birth of a Nejeret with the ability to destroy our kind absolutely was a damn shrug.

I was at a complete and utter loss for words.

"So . . . maybe this is a long shot," Kat said, breaking the tense silence, "but isn't it possible that this is just a coincidence?" Her focus skipped around to each of us. "Like, couldn't someone have made this—I don't know—two hundred years ago or whatever and Dr. Ramirez just stumbled across it and assumed it was for you because of your name and everything, but maybe it was really for someone else with the same name?" She deflated visibly, slouching back in her chair. "And now that I've said that out loud, I've heard how stupid it sounds."

"Not stupid," I said, giving her knee a squeeze under the table. "Just optimistic. It's good to be able to see all the possible angles."

I split my gaze between Dominic and Re-Nik for several long seconds, then settled my focus on the more ancient of the two. I was confounded by his apparent indifference to how this might've happened, but I put that aside for the moment. "While figuring out who did this is definitely a top priority, I think getting rid of the danger is probably a smidgen more important at the moment." As Dominic reached into his trouser pocket for his cell phone, my eyes snapped to him. "Do *not* call Marcus right now."

His dark gaze burned into me, his sharp features tense. "He needs to know."

"Not yet." I took a deep breath and set my jaw, preparing for a prolonged stare-down. It was a tactic that usually worked on Dominic on the rare occasion that we were at odds with one another. Not this time. As he inhaled to argue further, I cut him off with, "It's pointless to tell Marcus now. We're too far away for him to be able to do anything but worry."

I could see Dominic's determination wavering.

"We'll go back to the car and I'll sit in there like a good little Meswett until Neffe gets back, and I promise I'll tell Marcus everything as soon as we get home. But if you tell Marcus now, he'll demand that we return immediately, and Neffe won't be able to finish her research on poor little Tarsi . . ." I stared into his eyes, pleading with my own. I couldn't stand the idea of Tarset being frozen in time for a second longer than necessary. "Dom, please."

Finally, Dominic gave a single, slow nod. "But if we sense even a hint of danger, we're leaving immediately."

"I believe the only threat to Alexandra on this day is sitting on the table," Re-Nik said, pointing to the slender box with his chin. "Clearly whoever planted the watch on Dr. Ramirez intended for it to find its way to Alexandra, and we can safely assume that their objective was not simply to kill her, but to remove her from existence entirely."

I frowned. "Isn't that sort of the same thing?"

"No, my Alexandra, it is not."

I raised my eyebrows.

"Had you touched the pocket watch, in time, it would have been as though you'd never existed at all." He leaned forward, elbows on the table and fingers steepled together. "The past would have rearranged into a pattern absent of you entirely. And considering your recent trip into ancient times, anyone can see that the ramifications would be enormous." He nodded slowly to himself, his eyes squinted in thought. "But *had* you touched the watch, it would have taken quite a while to unravel the threads of your existence completely and weave those that remain back together in a new pattern, so . . ." He nodded again, more definitively this time. "It seems fairly obvious to me that you are quite safe right now, especially from whoever laid the trap. The deceiver has invested in this particular offensive." He looked at me, certainty written all over his face. "Killing you would be counterproductive, at present."

I blew out a breath and slouched back in my chair, mimicking Kat. "Well, isn't that a relief," I said sarcastically.

"Yeah, not so much," Nik said, his sarcasm matching mine. His eyes had returned to their natural pale blue once more, his features transformed to his harsher, standoffish expression. He reached out and dragged the box closer to him, then lifted the lid once more.

"Nik!" I all but shouted as he lowered his hand to the beyond-deadly pocket watch. "What are you doing?"

He glanced at me, his eyes steely. "Neutralizing the threat," he said, his hand hovering over the watch.

I saw a flash of quicksilver beneath his palm, and then a translucent film of pearly At seemed to wink into existence around the offending device. He'd encased the watch in solidified At.

I stared at the thing, eyes wide with wonder. The ticking—the feeling of dread, of revulsion, of wrongness—was gone. It was like the oxygen had been slowly draining from the room, but now it had been replenished and I could finally—*finally*—take a blissfully deep breath.

Despite my overwhelming relief, I flinched when Nik curled his fingers around the watch and picked it up. "Nik, are you sure—"

"It's perfectly safe now, Lex." He flashed me a devilish smirk and winked. "Promise." His good humor lasted only so long. His eyes widened when he looked at the back of the pocket watch, then narrowed to irritated slits. "I suppose I shouldn't be surprised," he said, flinging the watch back into its little depression in the case facedown.

"It's your name!" Kat exclaimed to Nik, having read the engraving upside down.

"No," I said softly. While the letters *N*, *I*, and *K* were engraved into the smooth black metal on the back of the watch, they didn't spell out "Nik." I sighed, suddenly very tired. "Not *NIK*—it says *KIN*." The same group who'd stolen the sphere containing Apep, his twisted soul. The same group who'd shot Dominic. The same group who'd turned Kat's mom against Nejeretkind completely.

I looked at Kat in time to see the color drain from her face. "You don't think it was—" She swallowed roughly, took a deep breath, closed her eyes, and tried again. "You don't think my mom was a part of this—of trying to—to *erase* you, Lex, do you?" When she opened her eyes, twin streams of tears streaked down her cheeks.

In that single moment, I didn't feel fear or worry or the urgent need to run and hide. Like Re had said—the danger, for now, was past. At the moment, I only felt a deep-seated sadness for the young woman sitting beside me. For the pain and guilt this was causing her. For the longing I could see in her eyes—that of a little girl crying out for her mother to hold her and tell her everything would be okay. For not being able to reassure her of her mom's innocence.

So I did the only thing I could think of. I slid out of my chair, crouched beside Kat's, and wrapped my arms around her, giving her what little comfort I could while she cried.

9

EXIST & LIVE

"Thank you," I said to the four other people in the Range Rover. Dominic had parked in the roundabout driveway, just before the entrance to the house, but I wanted each of them to know how grateful I was that they'd kept their word—and their silence, where Marcus was concerned—before we got out of the car. "Really—" I met each of their eyes, even Dominic's in the rearview mirror. "Thank you."

I glanced down at my hands, fidgeting with the hem of my shorts. "And, um, you might want to steer clear of the house for a couple hours." Passion had never been an issue where Marcus and I were concerned, and usually I viewed that fact in a very, *very* positive light, but that same passion made our relationship just a touch volatile at times. And I had no doubt that the conversation Marcus and I were about to have was going to be one of *those* times.

Neffe ended up being the only person to actually get out of the car with me at the house, Nik and Kat opting to remain with Dominic until he'd parked in the huge detached garage nearby.

"You don't have to come in with me," I told her as we walked up the broad paved steps leading up to the front door.

"I'm perfectly capable of handling him on my own." The tension tightening my shoulders and making my neck and head ache suggested otherwise, but I ignored it. Brave face and all that.

Neffe snorted. Apparently she didn't believe me either. "I'm heading straight down to the lab." She glanced at me sidelong. "It's soundproofed."

I inhaled deeply, but a sudden spurt of anxiety made me feel like I couldn't exhale all the way. "Good idea."

As I reached for the door handle, the knob turned and the door opened. I had to swallow a yelp. "Marcus!" I said too brightly. "We're back!" I leaned in and kissed him, and before he could wrap his arms around me in a full embrace, I slipped past him through the door and started across the entryway to the grand staircase. "I'm beat." I paused to glance at him over my shoulder, hoping my expression contained more *come-hither* than *holy-shit*. "Warm bath?"

His features were unreadable, his golden eyes equal parts black pupil and brilliant iris. In other words, he looked normal, for him. So far, so good. "Where are Dom and Nik?"

I forced a carefree smile. "Parking in the garage. Kat's with them, too." I shrugged. "Dom said something about a lesson . . ."

Marcus blinked, his face still expressionless. "I see." His focus shifted to his daughter, who had almost successfully made it across the entryway to the door leading down to her lab in the basement. "How did it go today, Neffe?"

"Fine."

His eyes narrowed minutely. If I hadn't been watching for it, I wouldn't have noticed. It was the first sign that he knew something was up.

Get out of here, Neffe! I did my best to relay the mental shout with my eyes, but one look at Neffe told me she was already on the same page. The last thing I wanted was for her to get caught up in the shitstorm that I was about to hurtle into headlong.

After all, she'd only been following my orders—and I'd had to remind her of her oath to me to get her to agree.

"What did you discover?" Marcus asked his daughter as he shut the front door.

"I think I've identified the poison, but it's too soon to tell for sure," Neffe said, patting her insulated tote and once again heading for the door to the underground lab. "I've got a few time-sensitive samples, though, so . . ." She opened the door and paused in the doorway, looking back at her father. "If I'm right, Father, I should have the antidote ready in a day or two. I'll let you know as soon as I know anything." It didn't sound like a question, but it was one.

Marcus nodded, just once, and his eyes remained on the doorway even after Neffe had shut the door.

"Marcus?"

"Tell me," he said without looking at me.

I opened my mouth, then blew out a breath and shut it again. In several steps, I was standing before him, my fingertips touching the barely-there stubble on his defined jawline. I turned his face to me. "Promise to let me finish before you say or do anything."

I felt his jaw tense. His eyes locked on mine, black-rimmed gold and blazing with intensity.

"Promise me."

He gave me the same stiff, single nod he'd given his daughter, and I didn't push him for more. In his present mood, doing so would be an exercise in futility.

I took hold of his hand, lacing my fingers through his. "Come here, sit down," I said as I led him across the entryway toward the foot of the stairs. He had an annoying habit of staring out of windows when we argued, and I was determined *not* to try to reason with his backside this time. I sat, pulling him down with me, and set my shoulder bag on one of the stairs a few steps up.

"Remember when I said I didn't sleep well last night?"

Again, Marcus gave that lone nod.

I sighed, searching his eyes. I hoped I'd made the right call by not alerting him earlier, but the danger had already passed. I told myself that several more times before continuing. The danger *had* already passed, hadn't it? "Well, it all started with this dream I've been having . . ." And then I told him. Everything.

To Marcus's credit, he kept his promise. He didn't say a single thing while I spoke. Hell, he didn't move beyond the steady rise and fall of his chest, the intermittent blink, or the slow tensing of his whole body.

As I neared the end of my recap, I reached into my bag and pulled out the box containing the pocket watch. "And here it is," I said, handing it to Marcus. "The watch is harmless now, so feel free to examine it to your heart's content."

I watched his face, his eyes, his lips, his jaw as he opened the box and picked up the pocket watch, looking for some hint of his anger level. He turned the watch over several times, then he set it back in the depression that had been made for it, shut the lid, and placed the box on the stair above us.

"Are you finished?" he asked quietly and, with a slow blink, raised his gaze to meet mine.

Shit. His pupils were so dilated that only the thinnest rim of gold was visible around the black. And I knew from experience that only two emotions caused such a physiological reaction in him—extreme desire and absolute fury.

In a lithe movement, he stood and strode away from me. He took smooth, purposeful steps into the nearby sitting room and, true to form, planted himself before a window, his back to me.

"Marcus . . ." Using the staircase railing, I pulled myself up to my feet but couldn't work up the nerve to follow him into the sitting room. "I'm alright. Nothing happened."

Silence. No words. No movement. Just stillness. Just him, staring out the window.

"And before you start ordering me around, I'm putting my own damn self on house arrest, so you can save your breath." Not that I was really worried about him saying anything at all right now. God, when he got like this, it was like talking to a statue.

The house's main floor had high ceilings, but all the space in the world wouldn't have been enough to alleviate the stifling tension mounting all around him.

"Marcus," I said, my voice hardening. I took a single step toward him, then promptly developed a severe case of lead feet. I repeated his name, irritation lacing my voice.

Still no response.

"Damn it, Marcus." My hands balled into fists, my nails digging into my palms despite their short length. "I'm fine, I've already agreed to stay put, so I'll be perfectly safe while you and your people hunt down these Kin assholes." I paused, hoping for some sort of a response. A simple sidelong glance would've been better than the cold shoulder he was giving me. "What else do you want me to say?"

"Nothing." The single word ratcheted the tension up to suffocating levels.

Mounting frustration got the better of me, and I practically shouted, "Is it that I didn't tell you right away? Is that why you're mad at me?"

"I'm not," he responded, his voice quieter than mine, but his words just as sharp. His shoulders rose and fell as he took a deep breath. "I'm not mad at you, Lex." His enunciation was precise, impeccable, and each syllable set my nerves more on edge. "I want to tear apart those responsible for the incident today . . . I want to feel their bones snapping in my grip while my hands are coated in their blood." He bowed his head, and his voice grew quieter. "But I'm not angry; I'm terrified. I want, more than anything, to lock you away in a cage of At keyed only to me so I know that nobody will ever be able to get to you. Nobody will ever be able to even attempt to hurt you again."

I held my breath for a few seconds, waiting to see if he would say more, then exhaled and crossed into the sitting room to stand behind him. I slipped my hand into his and leaned against his back, pressing my forehead against his shoulder. "That would be no way to live."

He was quiet for a long time. Seconds passed, maybe minutes, and we stood there, apart and together. We were always apart and together, it seemed.

Finally, he swallowed audibly and said, "But at least you would be alive." At last, he turned his head to the side and stared down at me. "At least you would exist."

Lifting my head from his shoulder, I searched his darkened eyes. There was a hint more gold now, but his pupils were still unusually large, not to mention uncommonly glassy. I'd never seen Marcus cry—hell, I wasn't sure the ancient former god I'd bound myself to for the rest of eternity *could* cry anymore—but I wouldn't have been surprised to see a tear break free at that moment.

"Oh, Marcus," I said, my voice hushed. I rose up onto tiptoes and leaned my forehead against his. "Even if they try something like this again, it won't work, because I know what that anti-At stuff feels like now. I could sense it all morning, I just didn't know what it was I was sensing. You don't have to worry about me being unmade or anything like that. You're not going to lose me to this."

Marcus closed his eyes. "But what of the thousands of others ways I could lose you?" His eyelids opened, his eyes blazing like twin golden suns. "Every day, I'm afraid."

I smiled one of those weak, joyless smiles. "I think they call that living."

"It hurts."

"I know," I said, my voice soft. And then I closed the distance between our lips and kissed him gently, then pulled away. "Now how about that bath?"

His lips curved upwards, and he kissed the corner of my mouth. "In a bit, Little Ivanov. We'll call an emergency Council meeting first. These *Kin* have gone too far."

I snorted a derisive laugh. "As the would-be victim of an unmaking, I couldn't agree more."

"I know he's disinterested in taking part in Council politics, but having Re there would be beneficial." I heard Marcus's unasked question loud and clear.

Sighing, I leaned my head on his shoulder once more. "I'll ask him."

"And he'll say yes, because it's you who is asking."

There was a hint of jealousy in Marcus's voice, just humming along the edges of his words. I could've called him on it. But honestly, it was nothing new and hardly worth the effort. I rested my chin on his shoulder and smirked. "I don't know if you heard, but I'm kind of a big deal. I've got sway . . ."

Marcus turned around to face me, golden eyes burning. "Yes, Little Ivanov." His arms slipped around me, fitting perfectly along the curve of my back, and he lowered his head, his mouth hovering over mine. "I'm quite aware."

His lips touched mine, a gentle kiss. A plea, or maybe a question. A reassurance. As his lips parted mine, he slid the slightest tendril of his ba—his soul—into me to caress the edges of mine as only a truly bonded pair of Nejerets can do. And for a few, blissful moments, the Kin didn't matter. Ma'at and the fate of the universe didn't matter. Only this kiss, this moment mattered.

Shakily, I let out a breathy laugh against Marcus's lips. "So . . . the meeting . . ."

Marcus made a displeased noise low in his throat. He kissed

me one last time, then pulled back and nodded. “Let’s gather the others. This is war.”

This concludes *Dissonance*. Lex’s story continues in *Ricochet Through Time*.

Sign up for **Lindsey Fairleigh’s Newsletter** to stay apprised of new releases and receive previews and other book-related announcements in your inbox.

GLOSSARY

- **Ankhesenpepi** Nejerette. Nuin's eldest daughter and queen and consort to many Old Kingdom pharaohs, including Pepi I and II.
- **Apep (Apophis)** Netjer or "god." One of two Netjers responsible for maintaining balance in our universe, the other being Re. Apep was historically worshipped *against* as Re's opponent and the evil god of chaos.
- **At** Ancient Egyptian, "moment, instant, time"; The *At* is a plane of existence overlaying our own, where time and space are fluid. *At* can also be used to refer to the fabric of space and time.
- **Ankh-At** Nuin's power. Includes (at least) the power to travel through time, to create and remove memory blocks, and to manipulate the At on this plane of existence.
- **Aset (Isis)** Nejerette. Heru's sister. Aset was worshipped as a goddess associated with motherhood, magic, and nature by the ancient Egyptians.
- **Ba** Considered one of the essential parts of the soul by the ancient Egyptians. In regards to Nejerets, the

ba, or the "soul," is the part of a person that can enter the At.

- **Bahur** Arabic, "of Horus" or "of Heru".
- **Council of Seven** The body of leadership that governs the Nejerets. The Council consists of the patriarchs of the seven strongest Nejeret families: Ivan, Heru, Set, Sid, Moshe, Dedwen, and Shangdi. The Meswett, Alexandra Larson Ivanov, is also an honorary member of the Council.
- **Djeser-Djeseru** Ancient Egyptian, "Holy of Holies". Queen Hatshepsut's mortuary temple in Deir el-Bahri.
- **Hatshepsut** (ruled 1479—1457 BCE) Female Pharaoh during the Middle Kingdom of ancient Egypt. One of Heru's many wives, and mother to the Nejerette Neferure.
- **Hat-hur (Hathor)** Ancient Egyptian goddess associated with love, fertility, sexuality, music, and dance. According to the Contendings of Heru and Set myth, Hathor is the goddess who healed Heru's eye. She is often depicted as a cow or a woman with cow ears or horns, and a sun disk is frequently cradled by the horns.
- **Heru (Horus)** Nejeret. Osiris's son, Nuin's grandson, Aset's brother, and former leader of the Council of Seven. Heru stepped down from his role as leader to function as the Council's general and assassin, when necessary. Heru was worshipped as the god of the sky, kingship, and authority by the ancient Egyptians. He is often depicted as a falcon or falcon-headed.
- **Ivan** Nejeret. Leader of the Council of Seven. Alexander's father and Lex's great-grandfather.
- **Ma'at** Ancient Egyptian concept of truth, balance,

justice, and order. To the Nejeret, *ma'at* refers to universal balance.

- **Men-nefer (Memphis)** Ancient Egyptian city. *Men-nefer* was the capital city of Egypt during the Old Kingdom.
- **Meswett** Ancient Egyptian (mswtt), "girl-child". The Meswett is the prophesied savior/destroyer of the Nejerets, as supposedly foretold by Nuin upon his deathbed, though none actually remember it happening. The prophecy was later recorded by the Nejeret Senenmut.
- **Neferure (Neffe)** Nejerette. Daughter of Hatshepsut and Heru.
- **Nejeret (male)/Nejerette (female)/Nejerets (plural)** Modern term for the Netjer-At.
- **Netjer** Ancient Egyptian, "god".
- **Netjer-At** Ancient Egyptian, "Gods of Time".
- **Netjer-At Oasis** The ancient, historic home of the Nejerets, deep in the heart of the Sahara Desert.
- **Nuin (Nun)** Netjer/Nejeret. One of two Netjers responsible for maintaining balance in our universe, the other being Apep. Also known as the "Great Father", Nuin was the original Nejeret and the father of all Nejeretkind. Nuin was worshipped as a god associated with the primordial waters and creation by the ancient Egyptians.
- **Old Kingdom** Period of Egyptian history from 2686 —2181 BCE.
- **Re (Ra)** Netjer. One of two Netjers responsible for maintaining balance in our universe, the other being Apep. *Re* was historically worshipped as the ancient Egyptian solar deity.
- **Ren** Considered one of the essential parts of the soul by the ancient Egyptians, closely associated with a

person's name. In regards to Nejerets, a *ren* is the soul of a Netjer, like Re or Apep, much like a *ba* is the soul of a Nejeret or human.

- **Set (Seth)** Nejeret. Nuin's grandson, father of Dom, Genevieve, Kat, and Lex, and member of the Council of Seven. Possessed by Apep, Set went rogue when the Council of Seven chose Heru as their leader after Osiris's death around 4,000 years ago.
- **Sheut** Considered one of the essential parts of the soul by the ancient Egyptians, closely associated with a person's shadow. In regards to Nejerets, a *sheut* is the power of a Netjer, like Re or Apep, or the less potent power of the offspring of a Nejerette and Nejeret.

CAN'T GET ENOUGH?

NEWSLETTER: www.lindseyfairleigh.com/join-newsletter
WEBSITE: www.lindseyfairleigh.com
FACEBOOK: Lindsey Fairleigh
INSTAGRAM: @LindseyFairleigh
PINTEREST: LindsFairleigh
PATREON: www.patreon.com/lindseyfairleigh

Reviews are always appreciated. They help indie authors like me sell books (and keep writing them!).

ALSO BY LINDSEY FAIRLEIGH

KAT DUBOIS CHRONICLES

Ink Witch

Outcast

Underground

Soul Eater

Judgement

Afterlife

ECHO TRILOGY

Echo in Time

Resonance

Time Anomaly

Dissonance

Ricochet Through Time

ATLANTIS LEGACY

Sacrifice of the Sinners

Legacy of the Lost

Fate of the Fallen

Dreams of the Damned

Song of the Soulless

ALLWORLD ONLINE

AO: Pride & Prejudice

AO: The Wonderful Wizard of Oz

Vertigo

THE ENDING SERIES

The Ending Beginnings: Omnibus Edition

After The Ending

Into The Fire

Out Of The Ashes

Before The Dawn

World Before

THE ENDING LEGACY

World After

For more information on Lindsey and her books:

www.lindseyfairleigh.com

Join Lindsey's mailing list to stay up to date on releases

AND to get a FREE copy of *Sacrifice of the Sinners.*

www.lindseyfairleigh.com/sacrifice

To read Lindsey's books as she writes them, check her out on Patreon:

www.patreon.com/lindseyfairleigh

ABOUT THE AUTHOR

Lindsey Fairleigh is a bestselling Science Fiction and Fantasy author who lives her life with one foot in a book—so long as that book transports her to a magical world or bends the rules of science. Her novels, from Post-apocalyptic to Time Travel Romance, always offer up a hearty dose of unreality, along with plenty of history, mystery, adventure, and romance.

When she's not working on her next novel, Lindsey spends her time hanging out with her two little boys, working in her garden, or playing board games with her husband. She lives in the Pacific Northwest with her family and their small pack of cats and dogs.

Facebook: www.facebook.com/lindsey.fairleigh
Facebook Reader Group: www.facebook.com/groups/lovelyreaders
Instagram: @authorlindseyfairleigh
Pinterest: www.pinterest.com/lindsfairleigh
Newsletter: www.lindseyfairleigh.com/join-newsletter
Patreon: https://www.patreon.com/lindseyfairleigh

Made in the USA
Columbia, SC
16 May 2021

38038970R10081